FROSTBITE

DEBORAH BLADON

CHAPTER ONE

RAELYN

I STEAL a glance out of the window of the craft store. I can barely make out the cars and trucks crawling along the street, maneuvering their way through the snow falling over Manhattan.

As I approach the checkout counter, I carefully place the green plastic shopping basket down.

"Miss Raelyn Walsh, you're back!" The gray-haired woman behind the counter exclaims with a clap of her hands.

The bounce of her feet triggers a ring from the small silver bells pinned to the shoulder of her colorful sweater.

I take in the picture knitted on the front. I can make out a cherub cheeked Santa with a pink nose and a reindeer behind him. A small Christmas tree dotted with colorful red, blue, and yellow yarn sits just above her waist.

I don't have to ask if she's the craftsperson behind that wearable masterpiece. Knitting needles are always in her hands when she's not helping a customer.

"I need more balls," I say, adding a wink to the words.

She smiles. "If you keep talking like that, Santa will put you on his naughty list."

That's debatable, but I do know that I must top the list of worst customers ever since this is the third time I've visited this store in a week, and I can't remember this woman's name.

She knows mine because I paid with my credit card the first time I came in. I don't have a reasonable excuse for forgetting hers.

"Myrtle!"

I don't turn at the sound of the man's voice calling out, but the woman standing behind the counter does. "I'll be right with you, Toby. I'm just helping Raelyn."

Myrtle.

I need to add that to my memory bank or the notes app on my phone. I know I'll be back here in a day or two, and I want to be better prepared.

Less than fifteen minutes ago, I raced out of the brown-stone my sister and brother-in-law own so I could make it here before Myrtle closes the shop for the day.

"Eleven and twelve." Myrtle counts out the clear glass Christmas ornaments I'm buying. "Is that all, dear? Do you need more paint? A new brush or two?"

I shake my head as I reach in the front pocket of my jeans for the money I shoved in there. "This is it for now. I can't promise that I won't be back tomorrow for more supplies."

She takes the bills I offer before she hands me back a ten. "You gave me too much. You get a discount for being a valued customer."

Myrtle is too sweet for her own good.

I take the ten and slide it into the left pocket of my black wool pea coat. "I'll use it to buy you a coffee tomorrow. How do you take it?"

"With a grateful heart and a smile." She beams. "One cream and one sugar. That's it."

I type those details and her name into my phone as she wraps the ornaments in gold tissue paper before carefully placing them in a paper shopping bag.

"I'm sorry I ran out of boxes." She gazes around the cluttered shop. "I have another shipment arriving the day after tomorrow. You can manage this, can't you? Your walk isn't far?"

"Two blocks." I smile, reaching for the twine handles of the bag. "I'll hold this close to keep my balls safe."

She laughs as expected. "For such a sweet-looking young woman, you're moving higher up that naughty list."

I tuck a strand of my long blonde hair behind my ear. "I'll see you tomorrow, Myrtle."

"Have fun tonight." She raises a hand to wave. "Don't slip on the snow on your way home."

I grin at the sound of the bells ringing on her shoulder. "I'll be extra careful."

———

LARGE SNOWFLAKES HIT my face the moment I step out of the shop. I glance to the right to see a woman dressed in a thin trench coat. Her umbrella is engaged in a futile battle with the wind. It's pulled inside out by a sudden strong gust.

She curses loud enough for half of Manhattan to hear before she shoves the now-ruined umbrella in a waste can next to a snow-covered bench. The curved handle sticks out, precariously teetering as she wanders off, trying to shield her face from the snow.

I set off behind her with the bag close to my chest. I can't risk someone dashing past in a rush and accidentally knocking me over. I need these ornaments to fulfill at least a few of my promised orders.

Once I've had dinner with my sister, Dexie, and my brother-in-law, Rocco, I plan on settling into their guestroom for a long night of hand painting ornaments so I can get the bulk of them mailed out tomorrow.

I tug the collar of my coat up, trying to shield my neck from the wind.

I didn't think to bring a scarf, gloves, or a knit cap since my sister's townhouse is less than two blocks from the craft store.

I knew snow was in the forecast, but I hoped that fate would be on my side, and I'd beat the storm.

I watch as the woman who trashed her umbrella waves down a passing taxi. The driver narrowly misses hitting the delivery truck in front of him before he brings the car to a stop close to the curb.

She yanks on the back door handle and slides in. The relief on her face is evident when she gazes out the window in my direction as the taxi's driver turns his signal light on, hoping someone will let him in the bumper-to-bumper traffic that trails as far back as I can see. It's not that far, given that the snow has now picked up and visibility is down to less than half a block.

I round the corner to Perry Street. I'm almost there. The change of direction should give me a reprieve from the snow.

It should, but it doesn't.

The bitterly cold wind lashes the side of my face, so I bow my head to ward it off.

I take a step and then another, cursing the fact that I didn't follow my instinct and go to the craft store an hour ago.

Instead, I wrote an email to my former boss wishing her well for the holidays and hoping that her New Year's Eve wedding in Brazil is everything she wants it to be.

My breath catches when the wind trails over my neck as it pushes my hair aside.

A car horn startles me enough that I glance to my right to see what the fuss is about.

Just as my gaze lands on a car sliding into the back of another, I run into what feels like a brick wall.

The bag I'm cradling close to my chest smashes against me.

Something warm sprays over my face, and I trip.

Forward – right into the arms of a man.

CHAPTER TWO

RAELYN

"WHAT THE HELL? You should watch where you're going."

His voice draws my gaze up. I look into his blue eyes before I glance at his hair. It's brown and mussed just enough from the wind to look stylish. Since he's bundled a gray scarf around his face and throat, shielding everything from his nose down, I can't see his expression.

I shake the bag I'm holding to hear the unmistakable sound of shattered glass.

Dammit.

"You knocked my coffee right out of my hand," he accuses.

Great. Not only am I now holding a bag of broken ornaments, but my hair is going to freeze in place because this guy's coffee landed all over me.

I swipe my fingers over my forehead. "You ran into me."

He dusts his hand over the front of his gray wool coat,

chasing away droplets of coffee. "No. You obviously weren't paying attention."

What the hell is his problem?

He looks into his now empty coffee cup and the plastic lid lying on the snow-covered sidewalk. "You're lucky I bought this twenty minutes ago. Otherwise, you would have burned yourself."

Other than a sexy deep voice and a face that is at least half-handsome, this guy has nothing going for him.

"You're lucky," I spit back, trying desperately to wipe droplets of coffee from my chin before they freeze. "I would have sued you if you burned me."

I wouldn't have. Accidents happen.

"Sued me?" The words are wrapped in a deep chuckle. "Listen, miss, you clearly weren't looking straight ahead. If you were, this never would have happened."

"Where were you looking?" I drop a hand to my hip. "If you saw me coming, you would have moved out of my way."

He ponders that for a moment with the draw of his brows up. "What's in the bag?"

I drop my gaze to the bag, shaking it again, so he can hear the damage he's done. "My balls."

Even though I can't see it, I sense a smile has bloomed on his lips. "Your balls are in that bag?"

"No." I shake my head. "Or, yes. Christmas ornaments. I just bought them, and you broke them all."

"You broke them all," he repeats my words. "Next time, watch where you're going."

That's it? No apology. No offer to replace the broken ornaments or money to cover the dry cleaning bill to get his coffee off of my coat.

Snow whips around us.

"I'm late," he says gruffly. "You're making me extra late."

I step aside. "By all means, leave."

His blue eyes hone in on my face. "Here's a word of advice…"

"Keep it to yourself," I spit back with a raise of my hand in the air.

"Next time, have your balls delivered."

I shake my head. I'm frustrated to the point that I don't care what this guy thinks of me. "A gentleman would apologize for running into someone. He'd ask if they're okay. And for the record, I am fine, but you ruined my work. I was going to paint those balls tonight, and you messed that up."

His eyes widen. "You paint balls?"

Apparently, the word '*balls*' is as amusing to him as it is to Myrtle.

"I hand paint Christmas ornaments and sell them online," I say before I realize it's none of his business.

He chuckles. "That's quaint."

What a jerk.

I hold onto those words because it's the holiday season and good tidings to all, or maybe that only applies to kind and decent people. This guy appears to be neither.

I count to ten under my breath and smile at him. "Standing in the middle of a snowstorm talking to you isn't my idea of fun, so I'm leaving."

He tugs the scarf closer to his face. "We finally agree on something. I don't find this entertaining either."

I let out a huff before I brush past him and start walking toward Dexie's place.

When I stop to glance over my shoulder, he's watching me.

I'm tempted to flip him the middle finger, but I don't. I turn back around and leave the rude grump behind me.

———

I TRY to sneak quietly into the townhouse, but the singing Christmas tree-shaped mat on the floor ruins that. As soon as my boot touches the corner of the mat, a chorus of Silent Night starts. I curse under my breath, knowing that the sound will lure my older sister into the foyer.

It works like a charm.

"Rae?" Dexie appears with her hair tucked into a braid. She smiles as she tugs the red apron around her waist higher.

I point at her growing belly. "Your baby is going to be huge, Dex. I think it grew since I saw you this morning."

She lets out a sweet-sounding giggle as her hands circle her baby bump. "I'm plumping up. I had to take my wedding rings off today because they don't fit. When you're pregnant, you'll look just like me."

I can't argue with that. Even though we're four years apart, we bear a striking resemblance to each other. We have the same color eyes and hair. Try as she might, Dexie has never convinced me to jump on the pink streaks in the hair bandwagon. It complements her personality perfectly, so it suits her.

My hair is naturally blonde and a few inches longer than hers.

My sister glances at the paper bag in my hand. "What did you get?"

"Frustrated," I huff. "I bought a dozen ornaments, but a man ran into me on the sidewalk and crushed the bag."

Concern fills her expression. "Did he knock you down? Are you all right?"

"I'm fine," I tell her with a half-smile. "His coffee spilled on me, but it was lukewarm."

She brushes a hand over my chin. "You could have been hurt."

"I know, but I wasn't," I say to reassure her. "The ornaments didn't come out of it in one piece though. The jerk who crashed into me didn't even apologize."

She wraps an arm around my shoulder. "This is New York. You can't expect anything from anyone."

I know she's right. Even if the man I collided with wasn't looking where he was going, it wasn't all his fault. I was distracted too. Placing all the blame on him isn't right.

"I'm cooking dinner." Dexie adjusts the collar of the cute pink blouse she's wearing. "I made homemade chicken noodle soup, and those butter-topped buns that mom used to make when we were kids."

Our childhood wasn't lacking for anything but a father. Our dad took off twenty-four years ago, right after I was born. Our mom saw to it that my sister and I were well taken care of. We weren't spoiled, but we had enough food, clothes, and love to leave us with warm lasting memories.

"I'll go clean up, and then I can help," I offer. "First, I should toss all of this broken glass in the trash."

Dexie shakes her head. "I'm sorry that guy ran into you. Was he hot at least?"

I shrug. "He had a scarf wrapped around him. I only saw part of his face, so I can't judge."

She smiles. "Judge what you did see. Hot or not?"

"Hot," I admit with a smile. "I'm basing that on his gorgeous blue eyes and brown hair."

"Sounds like me." Rocco Jones, my sister's husband, rounds the corner to the foyer. "Are you two talking behind my back again?"

Dexie nuzzles into Rocco's chest as he wraps both arms around her. "Never, my love. Raelyn met someone today."

Shaking my head, I can't hold back a laugh. "I didn't meet someone. He damn near knocked me over on the sidewalk. He spilled coffee all over me."

"Not exactly prince charming," Rocco says. "Some men in this city could stand to learn a thing or two about how to treat a woman."

"You'd be the perfect teacher." Dexie gazes up at him.

I'm surprised red and pink hearts aren't shooting out from her brown eyes. I've never seen anyone as in love as these two. I can only hope one day I find a relationship as solid as they have.

"I'll set the table." Rocco presses his lips to my sister's forehead. "If I haven't said it lately, I'm glad you're staying with us, Rae. Family means everything to us."

It means everything to me too, but New York City is a pit stop on my journey. Once the holidays are over, I'll be off on my next adventure, wherever that may be.

CHAPTER THREE

RAELYN

A NIGHT SPENT WATCHING sweet Christmas movies with my sister put me in a much better mood. By the time I crawled into the ridiculously comfortable king-sized bed in the guest room, I felt calm.

To pay Dexie back for the delicious dinner last night, I made a batch of eggnog pancakes for breakfast. They are nonalcoholic, although I did add an extra sprinkle of nutmeg for flavor.

There is little that is more intimidating than cooking for Dexie and Rocco. The reason is beautiful, kind, and lives across the street.

Marti Calvetti, Rocco's grandma, is a wizard in the kitchen. It's the reason she owns one of the most popular Italian restaurants in Manhattan. The first time I had a plate of spaghetti at Calvetti's, I confessed that it was the best I ever had. I made Marti promise to never tell my mom I said that.

Marti has been bringing food over on an almost daily basis. Since my sister met Rocco, she's been well-loved and well-fed.

"Are you going to head out to get more ornaments soon?" Dexie checks the watch on her wrist. "I can walk to the craft store with you before I go to work, or you could join me for the day?"

She's been joking that I should stick around Manhattan and take on a job helping with her purse line. Dexie Walsh, the brand, has grown by leaps and bounds since she launched it.

I ignore the offer to shadow her in her studio. "I have to get started on painting ornaments. I'm falling behind on orders."

She tosses me a knowing nod. "I hear you. I'm behind too."

I can't tell if that's a subtle hint that she genuinely wants my help. Since I know little about how to craft cute handbags out of leather, I make her an offer I know she won't be able to resist.

"I'll cook tonight." I smile. "How does salmon, parmesan-crusted potatoes, and a spinach salad sound?"

She rubs her belly through the fabric of the red and white print dress she's wearing. "It sounds like a dinner I'd really enjoy tomorrow. We have that thing tonight, remember?"

I sigh, hoping that the 'we' she's referring to includes Rocco and not me. "What thing?"

Her thumb jerks toward the front door. "We're going to that charity art auction. I want to find a sculpture for the foyer."

She mentioned something about that last week, but I was in the middle of chatting with a potential customer online.

The orders on my Etsy shop have tripled since Thanksgiving Day.

"I'm sure you and Rocco will find something perfect at the auction," I say with a smile, even though I'm secretly holding my breath, hoping that I'm spending the night here.

"All three of us will." She steps closer to me. "You said last week that you'd love to come, Rae."

I might have felt that way back then, but I'm in full panic mode now. I'm relying on the sales of my hand-painted ornaments more than ever this year. I was let go from my last job as the assistant to a sculptor in Brazil. Her impending marriage and relocation meant that she didn't need me anymore. Even though she gave me a severance check and paid for my flight to New York, I'm still looking for another position in a much warmer climate than Manhattan in December.

I can't be responsible for stealing the smile from my sister's face. She's given me a place to stay for free, and I've gotten to know Rocco better the past few weeks. Going to a charity art auction may help me find inspiration for my paintings, the large ones on canvas, not the miniature ones on Christmas ornaments.

"What's the dress code for this evening?" I ask with a grin.

Dexie glances at the blue sweater and ripped jeans I'm wearing. "Not that."

I let out a stuttered laugh. "Brutal."

"Wear your red pantsuit." She wiggles her brows. "The backless one. You look sexy as hell in that thing."

I cock a hand on my hip. "Why do I want to look sexy for an art auction?"

"Gorgeous men love art." She glances over her shoulder

as Rocco descends the staircase from the second floor. "Case in point."

I smile at my brother-in-law. "I'll wear the pantsuit."

She claps her hands together. "I can't wait for tonight."

"What's tonight?" Rocco questions as he slides a pancake onto a plate.

Dexie turns to watch him. "The charity art auction."

He shakes his head. "Shit. I forgot. I've got a meeting tonight, Dexie. It's a deal I need to make."

Rocco's life consists of making my sister happy and investing in businesses that need his money and expertise.

"Seriously?" Dexie lets out a sigh.

"I'll make it up to you." He approaches her with open arms. "I'll be home by ten."

Suddenly feeling like I'm in the middle of a conversation I should have no part in, I turn toward the staircase. "I'm going to finish getting ready. I'll see you both later."

"It looks like it's just the two of us tonight, Rae." Dexie wraps her arms around her husband. "Just like old times."

My heart tightens in my chest. Old times meant all the hours the two of us spent together while our mom worked three jobs.

"I'll see you tonight, sis." I turn my attention to Rocco. "I hope you have a great day, Bil."

Rocco smiles at the nickname. Brother-in-law turned into Bil shortly after they married.

"You too, Sil," he bounces back. "Stay clear of men who aren't watching where they're going."

"I intend to," I say as I reach the staircase. "I'll run in the other direction if I ever see that jerk from last night again."

CHAPTER FOUR

CALDER

"HURRY THE HELL UP."

I respond to my assistant's reminder that we're already ten minutes late for the charity auction by whipping my middle finger in the air.

He tosses one back at me and ups the ante by adding the appropriate words to the gesture. "Fuck you, Frost."

I ignore him as I straighten the navy blue tie around my neck.

I can't remember the last time I got this dressed up. There's a good chance that it was when I went to my older sister's wedding. Since that marriage collapsed three months later because her asshole husband couldn't keep his dick away from other women, I'd say the effort I took to get dressed that day was a waste of fucking time.

I hope to hell tonight is more successful than that.

I donated a piece of my art for a good cause. The funds it raises will become part of a grant for kids at a community outreach center. The jury is still out on whether handing them a basket filled with art supplies will benefit them. I'd vote *yes* because the tools and metal my dad gave me when I was ten-years-old steered me toward the path I'm on now.

"Why do I need to do this, Bauer? Don't I pay you a fortune to show up at these things for me?"

I've employed Bauer Knight for the past two years. I did it as a favor to his brother, William, who happens to be a life-long friend of mine. Bauer needed an outlet for his creative energy, so I brought him to my studio one afternoon to witness my process. He cleaned up the place, took a few calls on my behalf, and negotiated a more than generous price on a piece I was working on at the time.

I offered him a full-time job. He accepted on the spot, and we've been working side-by-side ever since.

"You need the exposure." He looks at his reflection in the mirror. "The place will be crawling with photographers. Try to smile, Calder. The brooding, tortured artist look is so last year."

"If that's true, why are you dressed like that?"

Bauer glances down at the black suit and shirt he's wearing. "It's my signature look at the moment. I'm working with charcoal again."

I envy that.

Bauer's talent reaches beyond one medium. The first day he walked into my studio, he was convinced that he'd make his mark on the art world with resin sculptures. That shifted to ceramic figures before he picked up a sketchpad and a piece of charcoal. The fluidity of the characters he drew was remarkable. It not only captured the eye, but the soul. He sold his first drawing a week later.

"Good," I say succinctly. "You should stick with it."

He rakes his hand through his dark brown hair. "I can't. I

have to follow the urge. One day it's clay. The next it's watercolors."

I pay Bauer well enough that he can do that, for now. If he wants to be taken seriously in this industry, he needs to master something, not experiment in everything.

He's got time. He's only twenty-four.

Six years ago, when I was that age, I was selling small sculptures on a street corner near Central Park. I accepted as many compliments as insults back then.

"As soon as my piece sells, I'm out of there," I announce. "If you're on board for that plan, I'll buy you a drink at Tin Anchor."

The promise of a free beer at his favorite pub should be enough to lure him out of the auction on my heel.

"I'll pass." He straightens the lapels of his jacket. "It's an open bar at this auction, Calder. I can drink as much as I want. I intend on staying until they push me out of the door at the end of the night."

That's a bad look for me, but I'll fall back on my usual excuse of needing to work.

"Use that time to chat up a few people with deep pockets." I grab my phone from a table next to one of the windows in my studio.

"Why?" He chuckles. "You've got orders for at least a dozen commissioned pieces that you haven't even started yet."

That pressure is what fuels me. If I know I have a long list of clients waiting for one of my sculptures, it keeps me focused.

"I'll give you a ten percent cut of anything you book tonight, Bauer."

His brown eyes light up. "You're fucking with me."

Shaking my head, I grin. "I'm not. If you secure anything

with a deposit, the ten percent is yours upon completion and delivery."

"Damn." He crosses his arms over his chest. "It looks like I'm working tonight."

"That's the spirit. Let's get this over with. I intend to be back here by nine at the latest."

"Dreamers can dream," he says as I walk past him toward the door. "Mark my words, Calder. You'll still be there when the clock strikes midnight."

"No fucking way." I glance at him over my shoulder. "When midnight strikes, I turn into an asshole, so I need to be gone by then."

Bauer lets out a full laugh. "You're an asshole twenty-four seven, so that argument won't work."

I smile as we exit the studio to make an appearance at the last place I want to be tonight.

CHAPTER FIVE

RAELYN

I'VE BEEN to enough charity art auctions to know that at least a few artists in this room have a hidden agenda. When I worked for Eleni Melo in Brazil, she'd donate one of her glass sculptures to every charity auction that asked.

Many considered her to be one of the most generous people they'd ever met. I couldn't disagree with that, but I knew a secret that none of them did. Eleni was well aware that if her piece garnered one of the night's highest bids, the people in attendance would want to know more about the artist.

That's why Eleni would look to her inner circle to lend a hand. She'd recruit an ex-boyfriend, a cousin, or in one case, her best friend to attend an auction. When Eleni's sculpture hit the block, her self-appointed bidder would get to work. They'd shut down any competition by calling out an exorbitant amount. They didn't care since ultimately it was Eleni who supplied the funds to purchase the piece. It all looked above board since the signature on the receipt was always someone other than Eleni.

I didn't discover her ruse until I stumbled on a shed on her sprawling property. Inside were dozens of glass sculptures that she had supposedly sold at auction.

I confronted her, and she laughed it off, telling me I'd never make it as a professional artist unless I learned to bend the rules. She wasn't the only one scooping up their own work for more than its value.

That was one of the reasons my heart didn't break when she told me that she was moving to Australia with her soon-to-be-husband. I smiled as soon as her back was turned as a shot of relief surged through me.

"That's disappointing." Dexie huffs out an exaggerated sigh.

I turn to look at her. She's dolled up in a black dress that hugs her belly. She's wearing three-inch heels. I held her hand as we descended the concrete steps of her townhouse since some of the snow that blanketed the city yesterday is still clinging to the ground.

I shoveled the steps clean as soon as I got back from the craft store this morning, but the wind picked up, blowing snow around to settle in our path again.

"What's disappointing?" I poke her side with a gentle touch of my elbow. "They don't have a pickle and ice cream bar set up?"

She laughs. It's one of those carefree laughs that I've come to love. It's been more frequent since she met Rocco.

"Calder Frost is auctioning that piece tonight."

I glance in the direction one of her blood-red fingernails is pointing. Those are courtesy of me. My time spent working part-time as a manicurist in high school paid off. "What piece?"

Her finger jerks in the air in frustration. "That breath-taking sculpture, Rae. That's a Calder Frost. I was hoping he would include a larger piece in the auction."

I stare at the sculpture. It's a piece of silver metal curved into a trio of waves. It sits atop a square black box that looks like it's also crafted from metal.

When I approach it, Dexie does too.

It's on a rectangular table that is draped in a red linen cloth. Next to the sculpture is a white card. I read what's written on it in gold ink.

Fly Away

Sculpture in Metal

Artist: Calder Frost

"Fly away," Dexie whispers. "What a perfect name."

I tuck a wayward strand of my hair behind my ear. My sister insisted on handling hair and makeup duties for the evening. She did a top-notch job on both. My makeup consists of a smokey eye and deep red lipstick. She gathered my hair into a messy bun on the top of my head. Dexie insisted that it was the right choice since the pantsuit I'm wearing is backless.

I told her it didn't matter because I brought a blazer to cover up from what I knew would be the chill in the air. Dexie ripped it from my hands as soon as we arrived at this gallery. She handed it along with her coat over to the woman at the coat check station set up near the entrance.

I cross my arms over my chest to shield the outline of my hardening nipples from the eyes of all the men who have taken notice. Why does it feel like we're standing in a freezer?

"Are you going to bid on this?" I glance down at the sculpture.

"I should." Dexie bites the corner of her bottom lip. "I

was hoping for something bigger, but this would fit on the mantle of the fireplace in our bedroom. I know Rocco will still love it."

My brother-in-law is a bit of an art snob. It feels like I'm stepping into a museum whenever I wander the corridors in the townhouse. Art is displayed from almost every medium, including a few sculptures. Rocco even purchased one of my oil paintings on my birthday last year. He said it was a gift for both of us.

"He'll love it," I agree with a nod of my chin. "I hope the bidding stays within your budget."

Dexie smiles. "All proceeds go to charity, Rae. Whatever I pay will be well worth it to see my husband's face light up on Christmas morning when he opens the present containing that sculpture."

Seeing as how I only got him a shirt with BIL emblazoned across the front, I don't have to worry about one-upping my sister. I hope that one day I can pay both Dexie and Rocco back for being so good to me.

I glance toward the stage where the auctioneer stands and the dozens of plastic chairs lined in rows in front of it. "Let's find our seats. You need to give your feet a rest."

Dexie leans against my shoulder. "This is why I like having you in New York. You take extra good care of me."

I reach for her hand to tug at it. "That's because I love you."

CHAPTER SIX

CALDER

I FOLLOW Bauer into the venue just as a woman spots me on the approach. Her hand waves gleefully in the air as a gray-haired man stands by her side, looking like a lost camel on Fifth Avenue.

Judging by the expression on his face, he wants to be here as much as I do.

"Mr. Frost." The woman waves more excitedly now. "We were worried that you wouldn't make it."

I pat Bauer on the shoulder.

He leans closer to me. "Mitzi Hemley and her husband Augustine. She's the chairperson of this auction."

I give him an extra pat in gratitude before I approach the couple. "Mitzi. Augustine. How are you both?"

Augustine mutters something that sounds a lot like "*fucking miserable*," but I ignore that and focus my attention on his wife.

"Stressed." Mitzi reaches for my hand, and who am I to deny it?

She squeezes it, and I swear to fuck she runs her fingernail over my palm in a circle as she gazes into my eyes.

"Has anyone ever told you that your eyes are mesmerizing, Mr. Frost?" She questions with a slick of her tongue over her bottom lip.

"I need a drink," Augustine announces to no one before he heads left toward a server holding a tray of what looks like half-filled champagne flutes.

I'm going to need something more potent than that to get me to the other side of this evening.

"I tell him all the time," Bauer replies to Mitzi's comment about my eyes. I have no fucking idea how he keeps a straight face.

She turns to look at him. "Aren't you handsome too? What's your name?"

"Bauer," he says, offering her his hand.

I'm left in the dust when he smiles at her. Bauer always has my back.

"Why don't I get us some champagne?" He holds Mitzi's hand close to his chest. "You can tell me what I can do to help with the stress."

"Do you think you can help?" Mitzi sighs. "I need something to calm me down."

"I'll show you some of my drawings," Bauer says with a wink.

Mitzi giggles as if she's just won the lottery. "I can't wait to see them."

Little does she know that he's literally going to show her a folder on his phone's image app that contains pictures of his charcoal drawings.

Looking up, I take note that the auction is in full swing.

Someone is about to pay six figures for a watercolor painting by Brighton Beck. I'd toss my hat in the ring, but I've only ever bought one painting. It's the one piece of art I own that I didn't create.

I approach the bar and check the email Mitzi sent yesterday with the order of items that are available tonight. If things stay on track, my sculpture will be on the block within the next thirty minutes. I'll be out of here and on my way back to my studio before I know it. I might as well settle in and enjoy the festivities.

———

AN HOUR LATER, I'm cursing the person who got into a bidding war with Augustine. For some reason, only known to the man himself, Augustine desperately wanted to get his hands on an abstract painting of Santa Claus.

I stood in the shadows watching the bidding war heat up. It took more than twenty minutes as Augustine inched his way past the other Santa lover by upping each of her bids by a dollar.

The fact that the painting sold for less than a hundred dollars should have been a sign to both Augustine and the gray-haired woman in the leopard print scarf that it wasn't worth the effort.

Augustine let out a shriek and jumped to his feet when the auctioneer lowered his gavel and declared Mitzi's husband the winner. The woman in the scarf stormed out of the gallery leaving Augustine to enjoy the painting.

I take one last glance around the room as my sculpture is placed on the auction block. The murmured whispers around me are a sure sign that it's going to eclipse the Santa Claus panting in price.

Thank Christ since I wouldn't be able to show my face in public again if it didn't.

The auctioneer calls out a starting bid of five hundred dollars.

At least a dozen hands fly in the air.

Bauer catches my eye from across the room. He's standing near the stage, facing the crowd. He gauges their reaction while I stand behind them. Rows upon rows of people dressed in their holiday best are seated shoulder-to-shoulder as they try to one-up each other to get the prize of the night.

Tonight it's the small metal sculpture I crafted over the course of a few days.

I smile inwardly as the auctioneer sails easily north of the five thousand dollar mark. If I were selling this piece myself, I'd price it at five times that.

More hands drop as the price inches closer to ten thousand.

When it passes the fifteen thousand dollar mark, two hands remain in the game.

One belongs to a dark-haired guy in a black suit. The other bidder is a woman. All I can make out is blonde hair with pink streaks running through it. My gaze wanders to the person sitting next to her.

I stare because her neck and upper back are a sculptor's dream.

It's exactly what I wanted to emulate years ago when I experimented with clay.

Bidding heats up with the amount passing the eighteen thousand mark.

Twenty thousand.

When it jumps to twenty-two thousand, the man's hand wavers. He lowers it before it shoots back up.

The woman battling him for ownership of the sculpture bolts to her feet. "Thirty thousand dollars."

Hell, yes.

I won't see a dime of that, but the kids benefitting from this auction will. I'm about to applaud her when her bidding opponent shakes his head in defeat.

The auctioneer slams his gavel down. "Sold to Dexie Jones for thirty thousand dollars."

I watch the blonde woman with the exquisite neck and back dart to her feet. She gathers Dexie Jones into her arms just as her gaze travels over the back of the room.

I take a step forward and then another for good measure because *fuck me.*

It can't be. There's no way in hell that the beauty dressed in red is the same woman I ran into yesterday.

I straighten the lapels of my jacket because for the first time, I'm about to introduce myself to someone who bought one of my sculptures at a charity auction.

CHAPTER SEVEN

RAELYN

"LOOK WHAT'S HEADED OUR WAY." Dexie elbows me harder than I think she intended.

I stumble but gain my footing when she grabs hold of my forearm.

"Just look." Her voice is more insistent now, so I follow her gaze until it lands on two men.

Both are ridiculously good-looking. The slightly taller one is wearing a black suit and shirt. The shirt is unbuttoned at the collar giving way to the sight of a sliver of his smooth chest, and a peek of what looks like a tattoo. His brown eyes match the color of his hair.

The other man makes my knees go weak. With his brown hair pushed back from his forehead, I get a direct view of his striking blue eyes.

I stare at him as he approaches. Why does he look so familiar?

"Dexie Jones?" The blue-eyed man directs his attention to my sister once he's in front of us.

"That's me." Dexie's gaze volleys between the two men. "Do I know you?"

The blue-eyed man extends a hand in my sister's direction. "I'm Calder Frost."

My sister, who is never at a loss for words, drops her mouth open before she slams it shut. "You…are you really him?"

She's tongue-tied. I'm in shock that she is. I thought Dexie wined and dined with Manhattan's elite on a weekly basis.

She's never told me that. I assumed based on everyone she's met in this city since she moved here.

"I'm Bauer Knight." The brown-eyed man extends a hand to me. "I work with Calder."

"It's nice to meet you. I'm Raelyn." I take his hand for a quick shake to show my sister proper handshake etiquette since she's still grasping Calder Frost's hand.

It doesn't work. She hangs onto him.

"I didn't think I'd get to meet you tonight." Dexie giggles. "When I noticed you had a sculpture up for auction, I knew I had to bid on it until I won."

Calder levels his gaze on me before he turns back to Dex. "I'm grateful that you did."

I stare at his profile. He seems so familiar. I met a least a dozen sculptors when I worked for Eleni, but this man wasn't one of them. I would have remembered him. He's gorgeous.

"I was hoping for something larger, but I love Fly Away. I already have a spot picked out for it."

Bauer clears his throat. "You were hoping that the Frost sculpture up for auction tonight would be larger?"

Finally dropping Calder's hand, Dexie nods. "I'm looking

for something grand to give as a gift."

"How grand?" Calder asks with a glance in my direction.

Why does his voice hit me that way? It feels like my body is lighting up just from the low growl in his tone.

I cross my arms over my chest. My nipples have tightened again, and this time it has nothing to do with the temperature in the room.

"Seven feet…maybe eight?" Dexie lifts a brow in question. "You wouldn't happen to have something like that available, would you?"

Calder exchanges a look with Bauer that I can't place. The slight cock of Bauer's brow and the smile tugging at the corner of his lip have to mean something. These men might make my sister's Christmas dream come true yet.

"I know that you can't rush creativity," Dexie goes on, disappointment wiping her smile from her face. "Raelyn is an artist. She's told me that it's not as simple as putting a brush to canvas. She needs to be inspired. I'm sure it's the same for you. Besides, your sculptures are in high demand. They must leave your studio the moment you complete them."

Calder turns toward me. "Raelyn."

I nod. "Yes."

"You're a painter?"

"Oil on canvas," I say, trying to sound somewhat professional.

"What are you working on now?"

I gulp at the question. I can't tell him that I currently spend most of my waking hours painting intricate scenes on glass Christmas ornaments.

"She's been working on…." Dexie jumps into the conversation.

"I just completed an assignment," I interrupt to regain control of Calder's impression of me. "I was the assistant to a sculptor. Before that, I worked closely with Lysa Trumell in London for over a year."

It's never the wrong time to namedrop. Lysa is a big deal in the art world.

"Lysa's eye is amazing." Bauer shoots me a smile. "I'm working with charcoal right now, and her drawings are incredible."

Calder keeps his gaze on me. "Who are you working for at the moment?"

"No one," I admit. "I'm in New York for a visit."

"She's visiting me. We're sisters." Dexie wraps an arm around my shoulder. "You probably already guessed that."

"I see the resemblance." Bauer smiles.

Calder finally directs his attention back to Dex. "If you want something larger, I'll make it happen."

"By Christmas?" Dexie's eyes widen. "Are you serious?"

"Calder," Bauer bites out his name. "We should talk."

Calder once again turns to me. "I'll need assistance in order to get it done in time. Raelyn can help."

Um…what? What is happening?

I have dozens of ornament orders to complete. If I have to help Calder, I'll need to cut sleeping out of my schedule.

"She'll do it," Dexie agrees without even a glance in my direction.

Before I can protest, I catch Bauer's eye. He shrugs his shoulders and smiles.

"Bauer will work out the details with you, Dexie. I'll get started on this in the next day or two." Calder rubs a hand over his jaw. "I'm looking forward to working with you, Raelyn."

I manage a small smile in response.

Something tells me that I'm about to walk into a lion's den courtesy of my sister.

CHAPTER EIGHT

Raelyn

I EXCUSED myself from the conversation with Dexie, Bauer, and Calder because I needed to find a corner where I could scream.

I didn't find one. Instead, I found a server who offered me a glass of champagne. I took it and downed it in one gulp before asking him if I could get something stronger.

He directed me toward a bar set up in the corner of the gallery.

I asked the bartender for a straight shot of whiskey, and he didn't disappoint.

He refilled my glass almost immediately after I emptied it.

Now, I'm wandering the crowded gallery looking at a display of oil paintings.

My body tenses as I feel someone behind me. I hope it's my sister. I can't fault her for telling Calder I'd help her. I know in her excitement to get Rocco the gift of his dreams, she didn't stop to consider that I have a lot of work of my own to do.

As long as I leave Calder's studio by six p.m. each day, I'll have time to paint the ornaments that have already been ordered.

"Which painting is your favorite?"

I suck in a quick breath. That's not Dexie's voice. The woodsy cologne filling the air around me isn't from the scent of her perfume.

Calder Frost is behind me.

"I don't have a favorite," I offer without turning around.

"Why not?" Calder asks with a hint of amusement in his tone. "I have a favorite."

I shrug a shoulder. "I don't."

"You're not curious about which one is my favorite?"

I spin around to face him.

I don't know if it's the champagne and whiskey or his face. Something is making my stomach flip around as though there are a hundred butterflies in it.

"I've never worked with a sculptor who uses metal," I say. "Do you really think I can be of service to you?"

He focuses his gaze on my bottom lip. "I know you can be."

"How do you know that?" The alcohol has apparently stolen my common sense.

Dexie is relying on this man to make an extraordinary gift for her husband. I should excuse myself before I say something I regret.

"I assure you that you can be of service, Raelyn. You're a talented artist, aren't you? If memory serves me, you don't just paint oils on canvas. You paint balls too."

The glass in my hand shakes as realization takes hold of me.

Oh my god.

Calder Frost is the man who almost ran me over yesterday.

He's the arrogant jerk who wouldn't apologize.

"You're him," I accuse while balancing the almost empty glass in my hand. "How long have you known I'm me?"

I shake my head. "That didn't come out right."

He steps closer. His eyes lock on mine. "When you stood up to celebrate your sister's winning bid, I saw you. I knew it was you right away."

My hand darts to my lips. "You knew when you told Dexie you needed my help with the sculpture?"

He reaches for my hand to uncover my mouth. With his gaze trained on my red lips, he smiles. "That's the reason I insisted on your assistance."

I work my way through that declaration word-by-word. I shake my head to ward off the fog that's taking over. I can't be drunk. I can't be.

"You look pale, Raelyn." He holds my palm against his chest.

Holy hell, he's rock hard under his shirt.

Tugging my hand away, I stop a passing server so I can put my glass on his tray. I have to cut myself off right this minute – no more alcohol for me.

"I need to find my sister." I glance around the room until I spot Dexie talking to Mitzi Hemley. "If you'll excuse me."

"Of course." He steps back to let me pass. "I'll see you very soon, Raelyn. Feel free to bring your balls. I'm interested in seeing them."

————

CALDER FROST THINKS my balls are beneath him.

Wait. Why did that sound so messed up?

The look on his face last night when he mentioned my hand-painted Christmas ornaments said it all. He doesn't see it as real art.

I get it.

Some people value talent based on the price it lures. Others, like me, see it more abstractly. If a work of art strikes an emotion inside of me, I consider it priceless.

Based on some of the reviews on my Etsy store, I know that I've done that for many people. If they open their ornament box each year and see my creation and a smile touches their lips, I've done my job.

I finish putting on a pair of black jeans. Since Dexie has already left for work, I feel confident that I can put in at least twelve hours painting ornaments today. If I accomplish that, I'll be on track to finish the orders I already have. Unfortunately, I'm probably going to have to stop accepting any new orders for delivery by Christmas.

My phone dings with the arrival of a new text message.

It has to be my mom. When she texted me last night, I told her I'd get back to her today.

I walk over to the bedside table and glance down at my phone's screen.

Unknown: *What time can I expect you today?*

I stare at the message. I don't have any appointments booked. I'm not meeting anyone for breakfast, lunch, or dinner.

I shrug it off as a wrong number and walk back over to the closet. I reach for a black and red plaid shirt just as my phone dings again.

I rush back over, wondering if it's my mom.

Unknown: *The best cure for a hangover is hard work, so aim to be at my studio within the hour.*

I read the message twice before I scroll through my contact list to call my sister.

She answers on the first ring. "Rae, how are you feeling?"

"Confused," I say quietly. "I think Calder Frost is texting me. Should he be texting me right now, Dex?"

She lets out a laugh. "Oh, damn. I was going to wake you up before I left, but I had a call from our pop-up shop manager in Philadelphia. I had to go into my studio to find an invoice for her."

I should ask her if that situation got sorted out, but I'm on a path of selfishness right now, so I stay on course. "Does Calder Frost expect me to be at his studio today?"

"Yes." The sound of a car horn in the background punctuates the word. "Bauer called me early this morning to say that in order to get the sculpture done in time for Christmas, Calder needs to start on it ASAP."

I bow my head because there go my plans for the day.

"You're okay with helping him, right?" Dexie asks. "I know we didn't discuss it last night. If I put you in an awkward position, you'd tell me, wouldn't you?"

I didn't say a word to her last night about Calder being the man I ran into on the sidewalk. I'm still trying to process that information myself.

"Dex," I say her name while searching for the right words to gently tell her that although I appreciate that she's letting me stay with her, I have to complete dozens of ornaments to fulfill the commitments I've made to my customers.

Before I can say another word, she does. "I know you have work to do, Rae. I'll do whatever I can to help with that. Rocco has made me the happiest woman alive, and with the baby coming, I want to do something extra special to show him how much I love him."

Guilt wraps its cold hand around my heart. I owe my

sister so much. Not just because I always have a room at her home, but she's one of the few people in this world who encouraged me to paint. If it wasn't for Dexie, I might not have taken that chance on myself.

"I'll get all my work done," I assure her even though I don't know if I believe it. "I'll help Calder with whatever he needs so that sculpture is in the foyer on Christmas Day."

"Thank you." I hear the emotion in her voice. "I'm on my way to meet a supplier. I'll text you the address to Calder's studio as soon as I get there. I can't tell you how much this means to me, Rae. You're the best sister in the world."

"No, you are," I counter. "I'll be waiting for the text. Have a good day, Dex."

"I will," she chirps. "Good luck today. I've heard artists can be a moody bunch."

I half-laugh at the joke because she has no idea just how moody Calder Frost is.

CHAPTER NINE

CALDER

I SHOULD BE past the concept stage of this sculpture I'm hastily doing for Dexie Jones. Instead, I'm staring at the door of my studio, waiting for her sister to appear.

I haven't been able to get Raelyn out of my mind since we officially met last night. That's a fucking lie. I couldn't stop thinking about her after we collided on the sidewalk.

There was something about her that made me want to stand in that snowstorm for hours just to stare at her.

Blonde hair, brown eyes, and a face that is beautiful, not just because of her bone structure.

As she gave me shit while snow fell around us, I saw both fire and kindness in her eyes. I saw grace and goodness.

I know she was holding back her anger.

She was right that night. I handled the situation poorly, but the message on my phone that lured my gaze down long enough for me to almost walk over her put me in a foul mood. It was from a delivery company apologizing for not getting one of my sculptures to its owner on time.

A knock at my studio's sliding metal doors sends a shot of adrenaline through me.

I promised myself that I'd do everything in my power to keep my cock out of this, but it's already stirring inside my jeans.

I suck in a deep breath and head across my studio toward the door, knowing that I'm about to come face-to-face with the beauty I can't stop thinking about.

Sliding the door open with a tug, I straighten my stance. "Good morning."

"Good morning, Mr. Frost!" Mitzi Hemley greets me with a smile and a cup of coffee in each hand. "I brought you a little something to kick start your day."

Since I wasn't expecting to see the woman again, I cross my arms over my chest. "What can I do for you, Mitzi?"

"You can take these hot coffees off my hands." She pushes both cups toward me. "Please."

I take them because I don't want to have to tend to her burns in addition to whatever brought her down here.

Stalking across the studio toward a table, I hear her boots tapping a beat behind as she follows me. "It's crisp out there this morning, isn't it?"

I wouldn't know. I live in the loft above my studio, so I haven't stepped outside yet.

Once I reach the table and place the coffees down, I turn to face her. "What brought you here today?"

She glances around the massive studio. "Bauer."

Naturally. She's as charmed with him as most women are.

"He's working from home today," I tell her. "I'll be sure to tell him you dropped by."

A frustrated noise escapes her. "I was hoping to buy one

of his drawings. I'm celebrating, after all."

I should be asking what the special occasion is, but I don't give a damn.

"My painting sold for more than I thought it would at the auction last night." Her entire face brightens with a smile. "Although I must say, I was somewhat disappointed that you didn't bid on it. Bauer didn't either."

Scrubbing the back of my neck, I decide I better ask because I've never met an artist without a fragile ego other than myself. "What painting was yours?"

She throws her head back in laughter. "The one my husband bought, of course. He battled my sister until the end. I thought they'd cap the bidding at fifty dollars, but it went for twice that."

Mitzi is an artist? I didn't see that coming.

"Congratulations," I offer, hoping this exchange is coming to a quick end.

She picks up one of the coffee cups and offers it to me. "Why don't you enjoy this? I brought one for you and the other for Bauer."

I take the cup. "Thank you."

"That boy reminds me so much of my grandson." She tugs the lid off the other cup. "He's a lawyer. Life keeps him busy in Utah. I haven't seen the dear soul in years."

Her sudden attachment to Bauer makes sense.

"Why don't you paint your grandson something special as a Christmas gift?" I ask before taking a sip from the cup.

It's lukewarm, but otherwise, it's not half-bad.

She opens her purse and removes a packet of sugar before she pours it into the cup. "Do you think he'd like that?"

"I think he'd love it," I say, not having a fucking clue whether her grandson will appreciate the effort or not. "You should go straight to your studio and get started on it now."

She picks up her coffee and swallows a mouthful. "I might do that."

"You should."

She takes a step closer to me, closing the distance between us until she's almost on top of me. "Do you want to know something?"

I stare at her because her lips are lined so far away from her natural lip that I have to wonder if it's bad eyesight or intentional. "What?"

"You're not nearly as bad as everyone says you are." She taps the side of her cup to the center of my chest. "I thought you were a grump, but maybe I had you all wrong."

"Maybe you didn't."

Just as I register the voice saying those words as Raelyn's, Mitzi jumps back in surprise at the interruption and in the process, the coffee inside the cup in her hand spills forward, splashing all over me.

Mitzi's gaze volleys between Raelyn and me. "Oh, my word. Look at the mess I've made."

Raelyn marches across the studio in knee-high black boots that apparently my cock likes because I feel myself hardening even though I'm covered in coffee.

"It was an accident," Mitzi insists as she yanks a ball of what looks like used tissues from her purse. She starts dabbing them over my gray T-shirt.

"Or karma," Raelyn says under her breath as she reaches us. "You're going to want to get that in the wash as soon as possible."

Stepping back, I reach for the bottom hem of the T-shirt and yank it over my head.

Mitzi's gaze falls to my chest, but Raelyn keeps her eyes trained on mine. "I'm reporting for duty, sir. What should I do first?"

CHAPTER TEN

RAELYN

IT'S TAKING every ounce of willpower I have not to stare at Calder's chest. I glanced at it when he was taking his shirt off.

He must work out, or maybe he's so rock hard because of all the physical effort he has to put into creating his sculptures. Either way, I'm doing everything in my power not to gawk. Mitzi has much less self-control. She's fanning her face with her hand.

"I'm very sorry about the coffee," she says. "I didn't mean to cause so much trouble."

Something tells me she doesn't regret it.

"I'm going upstairs to shower and change." Calder glances at the pool of coffee by his feet. "You'll find a mop and a bucket in the storage closest, Raelyn. Consider this your first task of the day."

Maybe this is my karma for finding so much satisfaction

in the fact that he had coffee spilled on him less than forty-eight hours after his coffee spilled all over me.

Mitzi turns to watch him leave. I do too, because Calder's ass in a pair of faded jeans is a sight to behold.

"Are you working for Calder?" she questions when Calder disappears as he climbs a flight of stairs.

"Something like that."

"You're one of the luckiest ladies in Manhattan."

I smile. "That's up for debate."

She lets out a chuckle. "If I were your age, I'd do everything in my power to keep that man shirtless as much as possible."

I don't respond because I have no idea if Calder can hear us. I'm assuming that somewhere beyond that staircase, he has a change of clothing and a shower. It has to be a bathroom, although I see one out of the corner of my eye next to what looks like a storage closet.

Just as I'm about to set off in that direction to retrieve the mop and bucket, Mitzi grabs hold of my forearm. "You did see what I did, right? His muscles are as dreamy as his eyes."

"I need to get this cleaned up." I reach for her hand to squeeze it. "It was good to see you again, Mrs. Hemley."

"You too, Raelyn." She reaches to grab her purse. "Tell Mr. Frost that I said goodbye."

"I'll be sure to do that." I nod.

"I met my husband when we worked together." Her eyes brighten. "Keep that in mind. You never know when love will find you."

It sure as hell won't find me here. Calder may be gorgeous, but beneath that beautiful exterior, a jerk is lurking, and I'd never fall for a guy like that.

———

MORE THAN FORTY-FIVE minutes after I finished mopping the floor, Calder comes down the stairs.

He's barefoot, wearing dark jeans and a navy blue T-shirt. It's pulled taut across his chest, and if I hadn't noticed his biceps and forearms before, I do now.

Being this good-looking and talented has to be a curse.

Maybe that's why his attitude could use a makeover.

"You cleaned the floor," he remarks as he nears me.

I don't know why he has to announce it since he clearly ordered me to take care of it before he disappeared.

"I had a few calls to make after my shower." He strolls around the table until he's facing me. "Then I made an omelet and had a cup of coffee."

Obviously, there is more at the top of the stairs than a bathroom.

"I live in a loft above the studio."

I nod. I won't tell him that's my end goal. Eventually, ten or twenty years from now, I want to settle in Manhattan with a studio just like this and a loft with wood beams and a fireplace.

"That's nice," I manage to say. "What's next on my to-do list?"

I might as well put on a happy face and accept that this is where I need to be until the sculpture my sister ordered is complete.

"Why don't you take a seat on one of the stools?"

I glance at the two stools next to the table. I did take a seat on one while I scrolled through emails on my phone when he was showering and enjoying a home-cooked meal.

I settle on the stool closest to where I'm standing.

Calder leans forward, resting his forearms on the table. "I do my best work at night."

I can't tell if that's a pick-up line or if he's serious.

"That's nice," I say again.

"Nice?" His brows perk. "Is that your go-to line when you're holding back what you really want to say?"

Um, yeah, Einstein.

I hold that gem in and smile. "I was commenting that it's nice that you do your best work at night."

He narrows his eyes. "Does it not make you wonder why I asked you to come and help me this morning?"

"No," I lie. "My sister said you needed my help, so I came to help."

Frustration tugs at his lips. He frowns. "I thought we could use this time to get to know each other better."

This isn't a date. I'm doing my sister a favor. "I think it's best if we focus on the task at hand. Christmas will be here before we know it."

"I already know a few things about you, Raelyn."

What? That I had crooked bangs for years that are forever documented in my high school graduation photos online. Or maybe he's referring to my brief time spent as a paid spokesperson for a watch company. My name will always be associated with the low budget commercials they produced. Those are just two of the treasures that pop up on the first page in any online search of my name.

"You have patience," he says, leaning closer to me.

"Because I haven't brought up the night you ran into me yet?" I question, holding back a smile.

"No." He shakes his head. "You didn't come looking for me even though I was gone for an hour."

"It was forty-five minutes," I correct him.

"Patience is something I value."

I value my personal space, and he's slowly invading it by sliding his muscular forearms across the table.

I stop staring at his arms and pin my eyes to his face.

It does little good because I'd be lying if I said I've met a man more handsome than him.

"You love your sister."

I nod. "Very much."

"You put aside your needs for her." He exhales heavily. "Why is that?"

I'm not going to deep dive into my relationship with Dexie with this virtual stranger, so I go for a shallow answer. "You said it. I love her."

"There's love, and there's sacrifice," he points out. "They are two very different things."

"Or one and the same," I counter. "Sometimes, a person loves selflessly. In that case, sacrifice feels like a gift, not a burden."

He studies my face. "I've never felt that."

I'm not surprised.

Sliding to my feet, I shrug my shoulder. "Maybe one day you will."

I wait for his response, but one doesn't come. Instead, he turns his back and approaches one of the tall windows in the studio. "We're done for the day. I expect you back here tomorrow night at eight, Raelyn. We'll work through the night."

I can survive on very little sleep, so I see this as a plus. "I'll see you then, Calder."

With his head tilted back in alignment with the rays of sun shining in, he raises his hand to wave in silence.

CHAPTER ELEVEN

CALDER

"WHO THE FUCK DID THAT?" Bauer's voice booms through the studio. "It's the middle of the afternoon. Are you working?"

I'm tempted to tell him to get lost, but I need him. I've spent the past two hours welding the base of the sculpture for Dexie Jones. Bauer is about to help me file down the rough edges.

My sculptures are imperfect in the sense that my clients know that they're going to receive a work of art that will never be replicated.

"I'm working. You're about to be working."

"Since when do you work when there's daylight?" He shrugs out of his wool coat and drops the gray beanie on his head on the table. "For the first six months I worked with you, I thought you were a fucking vampire."

I let out a laugh. "Go to hell."

"If I do that, who is going to help with this?" He scans the room. "Where's Raelyn? I thought she was supposed to be providing the extra hands on this."

"I don't pay you to ask questions." I stretch both arms over my head.

"I ask those questions out of the goodness of my heart." He pats his right palm against the center of his chest.

My eye catches on the sleeve of tattoos on his right arm. "You added something new."

He skims his hand over the inked skin. "When inspiration hits, I take it to the tattoo shop."

"You could bring some of it here." I point at the base of the sculpture. "I need to get this done."

"Why the hell did you take it on?" He drops both hands to his hips. "We both know you don't have time for this right now."

"Maybe I'm a nice guy."

He drops his hands to his stomach, bends over, and laughs. "Christ, you're a riot today. Did you get drunk at the auction last night?"

I wait until he's upright before I answer. "Dexie Jones is a potential long-term client. I can see her wanting another sculpture in the future. Maybe more. Why would I not make room in the schedule for her?"

"Is that how we're playing this?" Bauer perks a brow.

"That's how it is."

"You're telling me this has nothing to do with her sister?" He leans a hand on the table. "You're not doing this to get time with Raelyn? And before you answer, Calder, I saw the way you looked at her last night."

"She's beautiful," I spit out before my common sense can stop me.

Bauer's hands shoot in the air as if he's surrendering. "You're not going to get an argument from me on that. I've never seen you push work aside for a woman. That's all I'm saying."

"I need your help." I fall back on the issue at hand. "Now that I know Dexie's vision, this sculpture needs to get done as quick as humanly possible."

Bauer flexes both arms to show off his biceps. "I'm superhuman, so that's not a problem."

"In your mind," I quip.

"And in the minds of all the women who have tasted a piece of this." He lowers his hands to wave in front of him.

"When you're done admiring yourself, grab a file." I gesture at the workstation a few feet from where we're standing. "I'll take the left side. You've got the right."

"On it," he says. "One last thing about Raelyn, Calder."

I curse under my breath. "What?"

"She was checking you out last night too." He smiles. "Something tells me she's not torn up over the fact that she has to spend hours alone with you."

If only.

I can't read Raelyn Jones. Hell, I can't even read anything online about her because nothing exists.

I found that out this morning as she was waiting for me here in the studio while I was upstairs.

I was so hard that I had to pump one out in the shower just to focus after seeing her dressed the way she was. The plaid shirt she had on was unbuttoned enough to give me a glimpse of the top of her breasts. The jeans accentuated the curves of a lush ass, and those boots almost drove me mad. The image of me fucking her while she was only wearing them kept circling through my mind on a relentless reel I couldn't shake until I came.

My online search came up empty.

Hopefully, the fishing expedition I go on when she shows up here tomorrow night will give me more insight into the beautiful blonde.

CHAPTER TWELVE

RAELYN

I BID farewell to my sister just as she was crawling into bed. Dexie's pregnancy is kicking her ass. She's almost in her third trimester. I'm glad. I know that she's anxious to meet her baby. I've been bugging her to find out the baby's gender, but she told me that she doesn't want to know until the baby is born. Rocco is on board for that.

I admire their patience. If I ever get pregnant, I'll want to know as soon as possible.

I took the subway to Calder's studio even though Rocco offered to call me a town car when I told him I was going out to meet someone.

My brother-in-law has many connections in this city. Although he's fine navigating public transportation or utilizing an Uber or a taxi at times, he's most comfortable walking.

Dexie is the same. They don't wear their wealth for the world to see. They do good things with the money they work hard to earn. I suspect the sculpture Dex ordered from Calder is one of the few extravagances she's indulged in other than their townhouse.

As I approach the building that houses Calder's studio and loft, I look up. He occupies the top two floors. Light seeps out from the floor where his studio is located. The space above is dark.

My mind wanders to what his home looks like. Is it furnished in natural woods and dark tones, or is it a blank canvas that only contains the essentials along with a few of his sculptures?

I don't have a home of my own.

I've spent my time since graduating college living in London and Brazil. I feel at home in my sister's townhouse, but that's not a forever scenario.

As soon as I lock down another job, I'll have a new place to rest my head for a year or two.

Eventually, I'll find my way back here so I can be close to my sister and her family.

Just as I'm about to grab one of the door handles, Calder appears on the other side dressed in jeans and a white T-shirt.

I'm dressed almost identically, although I slipped a light blue cardigan over the T-shirt. I don't need my nipples causing a distraction tonight, and since I noticed a chill in the air in Calder's studio, I came prepared.

"Raelyn," he greets me as he shoves open the door. "You're right on time."

I'm early.

"It's important to be punctual," I say with a smile. "I don't like making anyone wait for me."

That was about as subtle as a freight train speeding down the track in the middle of the night. If he doesn't realize I'm referring to the waiting game he played with me yesterday, he's dense.

"Some people are worth waiting for." He smirks.

Why does that smirk make him hotter than he already is? If he combed his hair this morning, I can't tell. The messy hair combined with his cologne makes me want to reach out and touch him.

He looks past my shoulder toward the street. "I ordered some take-out. It looks like it's here."

When I realize that he didn't come down here just to greet me, disappointment washes over me.

I step aside to let him pass to retrieve the food.

He carries on a brief conversation with the driver about the snowstorm the other night.

As he wishes him safe travels, I catch a whiff of something heavenly.

His hand lands on the center of my back as he steps next to me. "I hope you like pizza."

I look down at the square box with red and green lettering on it. "Who doesn't?"

"Bauer." He chuckles as he motions for me to walk into the lobby of the building. "I don't know how he considers himself a true New Yorker. He won't eat pizza or hotdogs."

I turn and look at him. "What won't you eat?"

His gaze trails over my body from head-to-toe before he looks into my eyes. "I'd rather talk about what I want to eat."

A rush of heat courses through me before my cheeks bloom pink with a blush. "We should get to work."

He stares at me intently. "We should."

We stand there for what feels like endless moments staring at each other. The sound of the lobby doors opening turns us both in that direction.

A man in a wool trench coat and black slacks rushes past us in silence toward the elevator.

"Good evening to you too," Calder calls after him.

The man jabs a finger into the elevator call button just as the doors slide open. He boards it without a word to either of us.

As soon as the doors close, Calder looks at me. "Fucking jerk."

I burst out laughing, which lures a smile to his lips.

"Let's get upstairs." He turns toward the elevator. "We have a long night ahead of us."

CHAPTER THIRTEEN

CALDER

I'VE NEVER WATCHED a woman eat. Sure, I've sat across from my share of women while we've had dinner, but I've never paid attention.

For me, it was always about what followed the meal.

I've dated. Hell, I've been in a couple of semi-serious relationships, but nothing ever lasted beyond a few months.

I could blame it on the women I was involved with, but it's hard-as-hell to deal with me. I own that.

For one thing, I work at night.

That started years ago when I couldn't shake a bout of insomnia. I tried the obvious remedies, including mediation and CBD oil, but nothing gave me what I needed. A clear head so I could get at least a few hours of restless sleep.

Once I switched up my schedule, I found that I could sleep more during the day. I can catch a solid four or five hours in the morning. I did that today after Bauer and I completed the base of Dexie's sculpture.

Raelyn takes another bite of the pizza. A fucking adorable sound escapes her. It's a cross between a moan and a giggle. I take it to mean that the pizza is a win.

"This is so good," she comments as she swallows the bite. "It's hard to know where to find great pizza in New York."

"There's a place in Brooklyn you should try. I'm due for another visit. We can go together."

Her head pops up. "What do you mean?"

She's blushing again, but this time it's barely noticeable. I notice, though, because she's a vision. Everything from her long lashes to the natural pout of her lips is captivating to me.

"I mean, we could ride the subway to Brooklyn, walk two blocks, sit in a couple of uncomfortable wooden chairs and share a pizza."

"I'll pay half," she blurts out. "Since it's not a date, I should pay my fair share."

I struggle to hold in a smile. "Whatever works for you."

She nods as if my response is acceptable.

"Are you in a relationship, Raelyn?"

The pizza slice in her hand drops back into the box. "What did you just ask me?"

"Are you seeing anyone?"

She shakes her head. "No."

"Are you sleeping with anyone?"

Her eyes widen as her entire face goes red. "Oh my God. Why would you ask me that?"

I lean back on the stool I'm sitting on. "Curiosity."

"Well, in that case, are you?" she spits the question out before her hand darts to cover her mouth. "Don't answer that."

"Don't answer what?" I rake a hand through my hair. "Do you want to know if I'm dating anyone, or are you more interested in whether or not I'm fucking anyone at the moment?"

She closes her eyes and shakes her head. "Both. No, I mean, I don't want an answer to either question."

"Yes, you do," I press.

She locks her eyes on mine. "I said I don't."

"For the record, I'm not dating anyone, and since you and I are the only two people in this room, I am not fucking anyone at this moment. That's not to say…"

Her hand darts in the air. "Don't say you want to… you aren't going to say you want to sleep with me, are you?"

I shake my head.

Her gaze drops. I know disappointment when I see it.

I lean forward again, inching my hand across the table until it's almost touching her. "Sleeping next to you isn't what I'm interested in, Raelyn. Having you in my bed is."

She bolts to her feet. "You can't just say that."

I follow her lead and stand. "Why not?"

"We barely know each other," she points out with her hands on her hips. "We're supposed to be working on a sculpture for my sister, not talking about sex."

I drop my gaze to the front of her T-shirt and the outline of her hardened nipples beneath it. "Why can't we do both?"

"We just can't, Calder."

I crack a smile. "That's not a reason."

She takes a deep breath. "It would complicate things."

"What things?"

"Things," she answers.

She crosses her arms over her chest.

I do the same. "Let me make this clear, Raelyn. I'm very attracted to you. If you ever find yourself attracted to me, I'm available. You say the word, and I'll drop my clothes."

With that, I turn and walk toward the sculpture we need to work on.

Before I'm a foot away, I hear her whisper, "What's the word?"

I turn back around to find her taking another bite of pizza. She tosses me an innocent wave. "I'll be right there to help."

Fuck me. I want this woman. It seems as though this time, I'm the one having their patience tested.

CHAPTER FOURTEEN

RAELYN

"HOW DID it go with Calder last night?" Dexie asks as soon as the door closes behind Rocco. Even though it's Saturday, he's off to a meeting.

"Fine," I say, not wanting to delve into the details of that uncomfortable sex talk we had.

I only spent two hours at Calder's studio last night.

The majority of that time, I was holding the end of a tape measure while Calder measured a piece of metal over and over again. He finally gave up, told me I could leave, and locked the doors to his studio behind me.

I was in bed by midnight and up at six to get started on my ornament orders.

"Fine?" she repeats back with a fair bit of attitude in her tone.

I laugh. "That's what I said."

Dexie crosses the kitchen to grab an apple from a fruit bowl. "Are you two hitting it off?"

I catch the apple when she tosses it to me. "We're working on a project together. It's not really about us hitting it off."

"I'll take that to mean you are." She chooses another apple and takes a bite of it.

"Take it to mean we're not," I counter with a smile.

She studies me from across her kitchen. "It wouldn't hurt to have a holiday fling."

It might. I've never been the type to be devastated after a breakup, but I've never had a one-night stand or a sex-only agreement with a man. Calder Frost seems like a heart-breaker, and I like my heart just as it is – in one piece.

"I have work to do." I slide off the stool. "I need to work on my ornament orders before I go to Calder's studio later."

"I'll help."

I glance at her. "You will?"

"It's the least I can do." She sighs. "You're doing me the biggest favor in the world by helping Calder so he can get the sculpture done in time for Christmas. Tell me what you need, and I'll do it."

"I could use help with packing up the orders I've finished," I say, stepping closer to my sister. "It's easy. Package the ornament. Print a label. Apply it, and that's it."

Dexie moves to embrace me. "I can handle it. I'll even take them down to the post office and mail them."

I step back, resting my hands on her shoulders. "We'll do that together. Maybe we can fit in a quick lunch on the way back."

"Pizza?" She asks, her eyes lighting up. "I haven't had pizza in forever. Have you?"

Last night while I was staring into Calder Frost's eyes.

I keep that to myself. "Pizza it is."

———

I ARRIVE at Calder's studio at precisely ten minutes before eight. This is one of the few times I wish I were prone to being late.

The reason is simple.

Calder is standing in the lobby with a woman in his arms.

Her hands are pressed against his chest as she looks up and into his eyes.

The moment feels too intimate for prying eyes, so I spin around and face the street.

As traffic passes, I yank my phone from my coat pocket and scroll through my unread emails. I click on one, but I have to read it twice before the words of gratitude from a customer who just received her ornament order sink in.

I try to read another message, but I can't.

I don't understand why annoying stabs of jealousy are piercing my heart.

I'm not sure I even like Calder Frost.

Why do I care if he's just come from having sex in his studio with the brunette who is clinging to him? Maybe she's an ex begging him to take her back? Or perhaps it's the reverse, and he's the one about to fall to his knees to plead with her to give him another chance.

I suck in a deep breath and will myself to think about anything other than Calder.

"Raelyn?"

When I hear his voice behind me, my stomach twists into a tangled knot. He says my name slightly different than anyone I've ever known. He puts more emphasis on the 'l,' so it sounds lighter or charming.

I can't explain it, but I've come to like it.

I spin to face him because I can't exactly pretend that I'm not me for more than half a second.

The brown-haired woman standing next to him smiles. "I'm Magnolia. It's so nice to meet you. My brother told me about you."

I look at her eyes. They are the same breathtaking blue shade as Calder's. I shouldn't take comfort in the knowledge that she's his sister, but I do.

"I'm Raelyn," I offer even though she knows that.

"I'm getting married in six weeks." She waves her left hand in the air. The streetlights cast enough light that the diamond sparkles.

"Congratulations," I offer. "That's very exciting."

"So exciting." She bounces up and down in her brown boots. "Calder is going to be my man of honor."

Is that what he is? Is he a man of honor?

I turn to look at him. "Congratulations to you as well."

His expression doesn't change. "Raelyn and I need to get to work, Mags. We'll meet next week for more wedding planning."

She grabs his face and plants a kiss on his cheek. "I used to knock his Lego towers down when he was a toddler. Now, look at him."

I am.

Calder Frost is breathtaking with an imprint of red lipstick on his cheek and an almost smile on his lips.

CHAPTER FIFTEEN

CALDER

I DON'T KNOW if Raelyn's intention is to kill me, but I'm worried I'm about to drop dead.

The second she shrugged out of her wool coat, and I caught sight of the tight red sweater she's wearing, my heart stopped mid-beat.

I can't prove that, but there was an instant ache inside of me. That only worsened when she turned around, and I got a glimpse of her ass in the pair of faded, torn jeans she's wearing.

The knee-high black boots are back, which isn't helping my current cock situation.

I'm rock hard.

Thank Christ I'm standing behind the sculpture.

Her gaze travels over my jeans and the black sweater I'm wearing. Approval dances in her eyes and grazes her lips when she softly smiles.

"What's on the agenda tonight?"

I want to answer with what first springs to mind. Fucking - raw, uninhibited, tear the sheets apart fucking.

"I'm going to work on the sculpture," I answer with the aid of my brain, not my dick.

Her hands drop to her hips. "What am I going to do?"

Sit on my face?

Drop to your knees?

Touch your pussy for me?

"Paint," I answer, holding on to the last bit of self-control I have.

She shifts her gaze to the sculpture. "That needs to be painted?"

Hell, no. I wouldn't let paint within ten feet of anything I create. The natural inconsistencies in the metal are what add depth to my sculptures.

"No, that." I point at a workstation I set up earlier.

I deliberately set it up behind me so I could witness her reaction. I'm not disappointed.

I see the surprise in her eyes when her hands dart to her chest. She smiles. It's the most beautiful goddamn thing I've ever seen in my life.

"Calder?" My name escapes her in a strangled sigh.

"Yes?" I answer because I'm not going to steer this conversation. I want her to do that.

"Did you get all of that for me?"

I nod. "Do I look like the type of guy who paints balls?"

She lets out a light laugh. "No."

She steps toward me, and for a brief moment, I think she's going to wrap her arms around me and kiss me. What I wouldn't give for a taste of those ruby red lips.

But she walks around me toward the table that now doubles as a workstation.

When she reaches it, she takes a full minute to look everything over. "I can't believe that you did this."

With my hands shoved in the front pocket of my jeans, I stalk toward her. The urge to touch her is real.

I have no idea why this woman makes me feel things, but she does, and if I can do something to make her life easier, I'll do it.

She turns to face me. We're no more than six inches apart. "You bought so many ornaments and all that paint. I paint with acrylic on these. Oil on canvas."

I point at the table. "Use the acrylic for the balls, and if you feel inspired, there are some canvases in the storage room. I bought one of every size. I can dig up an easel too. Bauer has one or two around here somewhere."

Her eyes find mine. "Why did you do this? I'm supposed to be here to help you with the sculpture."

"You are helping," I admit. "You create here, and I'll create there."

Her lips part slightly.

"I fucked up those ornaments when I ran into you." I pat my chest. "My ego apologizes for being a raging asshole that night."

She laughs. "You admit it was your fault?"

"No." I laugh too. "I admit that I wasn't a nice guy after it happened. I trust this shows how much I regret that."

"It does."

I'm grateful for that. It's important to me that she knows that if I could change the way I acted that night, I would.

"So, I'll work on the ornaments while you work on the sculpture?"

"Unless you want to pack it all up and take it home." I raise a brow. "I can't promise that you won't run into another guy who isn't paying attention to where he's walking."

"Are you admitting that…"

I stop her on the second try to get me to admit. "I'm admitting that I'd like you to stay, but the decision is on you."

She runs the tip of her tongue over her bottom lip.

My cock thanks her by rising to attention.

"I think I'll stay." She jerks her thumb over her shoulder. "The lights you set up are better than what I have to work with at Dexie's place."

We both know that's not the reason she's staying, but I'll take it.

All I want is more time with her.

CHAPTER SIXTEEN

RAELYN

PAINTING ORNAMENTS, while a shirtless Calder Frost is behind you, is not easy.

An hour into his work, Calder yanked the sweater he was wearing over his head, complaining that he was too hot.

He has no idea how hot he is.

It's been two hours since his sweater was dropped on the floor, and I've spent at least half of that time stealing glimpses of his body.

I've seen attractive men shirtless before, but Calder takes it to another level.

"Do you need anything, Raelyn?"

His voice surges through me, sending goose bumps pebbling up my arms.

I stand and face him.

I should have remained sitting because this is almost too much.

His hands are on his hips. His hair is even messier than

earlier, and sweat is beading on his forehead and muscular chest.

I have to be dreaming this.

A small voice somewhere deep inside of me wants me to blurt out the word, *you*, but I can't.

"Water?" I mumble.

He rakes his hand through his hair. I stare in awe at his bulging bicep.

"Water it is." He nods before he starts on a sprint toward the staircase.

All I need to do is follow him. I could drop my sweater, my T-shirt, and my jeans on the way so that the only thing between us would be his jeans and my bra and panties.

I've never done anything like that, but I've never met a man like him.

This palpable desire I feel for him is overwhelming and unrelenting.

I hear him coming back down the stairs before I see him.

He stalks across his studio with an open bottle of water. When he reaches my workstation, he shoves it into my hand. "For you."

I take a swallow and then another, but it does nothing to take an edge off the heat.

"It's hot as hell in here, isn't it?" He skims his palm over his toned stomach.

"I'd be nude if you weren't here."

I choke on the mouthful of water I'm trying to swallow.

"Are you all right?" He asks with a grin. "Did I say something wrong?"

"You work in the nude?"

His hand drops to cover the front of his jeans. "Not when I'm welding."

My gaze follows the path of his hand. When he moves it, I can see the outline of his erection through the denim.

"Are you welding now?" I ask without thinking.

He chuckles. "Is that a request for me to drop my pants?"

I shake my head. "No. Oh, no. I didn't mean that."

"Or you did." His fingers find the buckle of his jeans. He unfastens it.

"You're not going to get naked right now, are you?"

I hear the hint of excitement mixed in with apprehension in my tone. He must hear it too, because he smirks. "Not unless you are."

I take another drink from the water bottle. This is way too intense. I need to lighten the mood now. "We haven't even kissed yet."

Why the hell did I say *that*?

His gaze drops to my lips. "Kiss me."

I take a step back. My ass hits the side of the workstation and the lone ornament I painted rolls off the edge, shattering on the concrete floor.

"Fuck me," I mutter under my breath.

"That would be my pleasure," he quips.

"I worked hard on that." I point at the broken glass. "I can't believe I broke it."

He looks down at the floor. "It was beautiful, Raelyn. You're very talented."

That surprises me enough that I look up and into his face.

"I mean it." He exhales. "From what I saw, you're gifted."

"You're just saying that," I accuse. "You didn't even get a good look at it."

"Like hell, I didn't." He chuckles. "I've walked up behind you at least twenty times in the last two hours. I saw the ornament. It was beautiful."

Was. Now it's nothing. Broken. Shattered. It's everything I don't want my heart to become.

"You don't think my work is frivolous?" I ask with a perched brow.

"Your work reminds me of a painting." He scrubs the back of his neck with his hand. "I bought it a year ago. It's haunting in its beauty. It's the only piece of artwork I own that I didn't have a hand in creating. Until now, that is. I'd like to commission you to paint an ornament for me. If you put a rush on it, I'll pay you triple of what you usually charge."

"You're joking." I laugh it off. "Why would someone like you want one of my ornaments?"

His hand jumps to my chin. The feeling is electric. Every cell in my body comes to life. "I'm serious. I want one, so I'll always see you when I look at it."

Caution needs to be thrown to the wind sometimes, so I do it.

For the first time in my life, I let fate take hold, and I tilt my head, lean closer, and press my lips to his.

CHAPTER SEVENTEEN

CALDER

I TAKE Raelyn's mouth in a lush kiss. Parting her lips with my tongue, I taste more. I want more.

My hands move. I slide one over her shoulder to cup the back of her neck. The other settles on her lower back just above her curvy ass. Fuck, I want a handful of that.

She purrs into the kiss, and I hold her tighter. Cradling her body against mine, I don't care that she feels how hard I am. Hell, it's all because of her.

I have never felt this desperate need for a woman.

She inches back from the kiss until her beautiful brown eyes meet mine. "Do you always kiss like that?"

I steal another. This one is slow and makes my knees go weak. She tugs my bottom lip between her teeth as we break apart.

"No," I say with whatever breath is left in my body.

"No?" she repeats with a tilt of her head.

"No, I don't always kiss like that."

"Oh." Her lips form a perfect circle. "How do you usually kiss?"

"Like it's just a kiss."

Her eyelids flutter. "Isn't this just a kiss?"

I press my lips against the corner of her mouth and chuckle. "You know damn well it isn't."

She nods. "I know."

I pull back far enough that I can look at her face. "I want you, Raelyn. If I haven't made that clear, and I'm pretty damn sure I have, I want you."

"You want me?" she asks with her eyes wide.

If she wants me to spell it out, I have no problem with that. "I want to strip you bare and taste you. I want to fuck you, and then I want those beautiful lips wrapped around my dick."

She stumbles back, but my arms are wrapped so tightly around her that she barely makes it half a step. "That's a lot."

I shake my head. "It's not enough. I want it all again and again."

Her gaze wanders to my chest. "I've never…"

"You're not a virgin," I say with confidence. "Your kiss tells me that."

She smiles. "No, of course not. I was going to say I've never had a fling."

"A fling?" I parrot the words back. "Is that what you think this is? We'll fuck and forget each other once we've both had enough?"

She nods in silence.

I pull her closer. My hand edges down her back to her ass. I grab it roughly, tugging her against me, so she feels how hard I am. "I will never get enough of you."

Her eyes search mine for something. If she thinks I'm bullshitting her, I'll prove her wrong. I don't believe in love at first sight, and in my experience, lust at first sight is purely physical, and the intense attraction disappears after the first touch.

I've never felt a connection like this before. I like her. I admire her need to help others. *This* can become something bigger than both of us with time.

"Let me take you out for dinner tomorrow, or I guess it's tonight."

The words surprise me as much as they do her. I want to hoist her over my shoulder and carry her up to my bed, but I want something else more. I want her to trust me. I want her to feel that she knows me well enough that she'll share more of herself with me.

The corners of her mouth edge up into a smile. "I'd like that."

"It's a date." I squeeze her ass one last time. "I'll pick you up at eight?"

Her hands slide from my shoulders to my chest. "I'll meet you here."

I kiss her again. Slowly, almost painfully, because I know this is my last taste of her tonight.

She smiles when her lips leave mine.

"Go home and get some sleep, Raelyn." I press my lips to her forehead. "I'll call a car to take you home."

"I'll get an Uber." She looks into my eyes. "Thank you again for all the art supplies, Calder."

I nod. I should be thanking her for every kiss she's given me tonight.

"I'll see you later." She winks. "Since it's already tomorrow."

I watch her walk out of my studio, taking a little piece of my heart with her.

TWO HOURS LATER, I rub my forehead as I sit at Raelyn's workstation. I took a shower and chased sleep by getting into my bed. It didn't come, so I'm back in my studio, staring at the broken shards of an exquisite work of art.

I've tried to piece it back together. I've realized that it's impossible, but what I've managed to connect has shown me that Raelyn paints from her heart. The ornament scene is of a mountain with a fresh stream flowing from the snow-peaked caps.

It's not as simple as that, but the purity of the brush strokes is flawless.

She created this in the span of a couple of hours. It's incredible.

A sound behind me draws my gaze over my shoulder. It's nearing three a.m., so unless that's Raelyn strolling back into my studio to spend the night with me, I'm not interested in who is behind the door sliding it open.

William, Bauer's older brother and my best friend shoots me a smile as he enters the studio. He pockets the keys he used to enter.

It's the middle of the night to the rest of Manhattan, but William looks like he just left the tailors. He's wearing one of his custom-made three-piece suits. His brown hair is cut to perfection, and the wool overcoat draped over his forearm is likely Italian made just for him.

"Calder!" he calls out. "You need me."

Pushing to my feet, I laugh at that. "Like hell, I do. Why are you here?"

"Bauer said you met someone." He drops his overcoat on a chair near the studio door. "Raelyn. Tell me about her."

"Why?"

"So I can help you not screw this the fuck up." He perks a dark brow.

William's job is to help men. He's an advisor of sorts. He counsels wealthy men in New York to become the best they can be. I may not be hitting the nail directly on the head. William's always been vague about what he does to earn a living.

"Don't you have a woman to charm?" I ask with a smile. "They must be lining up to jump all over you."

"They are," he says with a straight face. "We're not talking about who wants me. I'm here because you want someone."

"She wants me too."

His brown eyes narrow. "You know this how?"

"We kissed."

A smile perks the corner of his mouth. "That's a good sign. You like her, don't you? Bauer said there's a spark between you two."

"Bauer may feel something, but he's not my type," I deadpan.

"A joke and a smile." He pats me on the cheek. "I already like this woman. Don't drive her away, Calder. If she's good for you, break down those walls and let her in."

"I need those walls to create sculptures," I half-joke.

I've always used my inner demons as fuel for my work. Most of that is related to my grandparents' deaths and my regret that I didn't see them more when I had the chance. I'm not holding tightly to any of my past pain, but I'll dive back into it if I need the mood shift to find my muse.

"You need a hammer, some metal, and a few other tools." He points out. "Let her goodness seep into you, Calder. There's inspiration in that."

CHAPTER EIGHTEEN

RAELYN

I CARRY my entire wardrobe with me as I travel the world. Usually, if I buy something new to wear, I'll donate an older piece to charity. Today, I'm looking at what I have available.

Calder has already seen me in the red jumpsuit, so my choices are limited to a black dress, a red dress, or a white one. Because it's the dead of winter, I opt for the black one.

It has a plunging neckline, and the bottom hem falls just below my knees.

Paired with my black heels, I'll look elegant. That's the look I'm going for tonight, even though Calder didn't mention where we'd be dining.

There's a knock on the guestroom door. Before I can say a word, my sister wanders in dressed in what looks like pink pajamas.

"I came to see if you wanted to make popcorn and watch a movie, but it looks like you have a date." She eyes me from head-to-toe.

I could lie, but where the hell would I be going dressed like this besides a date?

"I have a date," I affirm with a nod.

Settling on the corner of the bed, she sighs. "With who?"

I toss her a look that must say it all because she squeals.

"You're going out with Calder?" She covers her mouth with her hand.

Rocco is somewhere inside this townhouse, and since we are still trying to keep the sculpture under wraps, I wince. "Don't say his name, Dex."

"Calder Frost?" she whispers. "Are you having dinner with him?"

I nod.

She jumps to her feet, wobbles for a second, but then finds her balance. "I like him, Rae. He's perfect for you."

I should agree, but the fact that I only just met him scares the hell out of me.

"It's just dinner," I remind her. "We're probably going to talk about the sculpture."

She glances over her shoulder. "That doesn't look like a business dinner dress. It looks more like a rip-this-from-my-body-and-ravage-me dress."

I stifle a laugh. "What the hell?"

"You should sleep with him."

I shake my head. "We're not having this discussion."

"Why not?" She kicks the toe of one of her pink slippers against the bed frame. "The sex would be mind-blowing."

I can feel my cheeks blush as I bow my head. "You don't know that. You can't judge a man's performance in bed based on his looks."

"Yes, you can." Straightening her back, she stands taller. "Look at Rocco. He's a beast in bed, and he's the most handsome man on earth."

I'd debate that last statement with her because I happen to think Calder holds that title.

"I'm not going to bed with him tonight, " I insist. "I'm having dinner, and then I'll be back."

"I won't wait up." She rubs her chin. "Do you want to know why?"

"Because you're very pregnant and exhausted?" I joke.

"No," she says with a straight face. "It's because you're going to spend the night with him. It's happening, sis. Brace yourself."

I let out a laugh. "Brace myself?"

She nods in silence.

I steal a glance at my phone's screen. "I need to go. I'm meeting Calder at eight."

"Use a condom or condoms." She pats her belly. "You may be ready for a wild night of fun, but you're not ready for this."

Moving forward, I kiss her cheek before I run a hand over her swollen stomach. "Sleep well, baby Jones, and you too, Dex."

"I hope you don't get a wink of sleep tonight." She kisses my forehead. "I also hope you can't walk straight tomorrow."

"You're something else," I say as I breeze past her on my way to get a coat. "I'll see you in the morning."

"Or not," she quips. "You might still have your hands full."

————

AS SOON AS I step into the lobby of Calder's building, he's exiting the elevator.

I sigh in relief when I see that he's dressed for the night in a suit and tie. The suit is dark gray. The shirt and tie are blue.

He looks gorgeous as he approaches me with a smile on his face.

"You look amazing, Raelyn."

He's judging that only by the skirt of my dress. I've bundled myself in my wool coat since the forecast is calling for snow once again.

"I reserved a table at Nova."

All I know about the restaurant is that my sister loves their food. She's raved about it more than once. "That sounds great."

He glances over my shoulder. "I ordered a car and driver to take us there. I don't see them yet."

Inching closer to him, I gaze up at his face. "What should we do until they get here?"

His eyes linger on my scarlet lips. "Do you know how fucking hot that red lipstick is?"

"Very hot?" I question with a smile.

He drags his finger over my chin, tilting my head up slightly. "Hotter than that."

I lean closer, resting both hands on his shirt. "Is that a good thing?"

Nodding, he tilts his head. "Kiss me, and I'll tell you."

Just as I move to press my lips to his, a car horn wails outside. We both turn to look.

"That driver's timing is shit," Calder says before he gives me a quick kiss. "Promise me that we'll continue this after dinner."

That's a promise I shouldn't make, but I do. "I promise."

"I'll hold you to that." He reaches for my hand. "Follow me."

I do, happily knowing that tonight may be the start of something life-changing for me.

CHAPTER NINETEEN

CALDER

IF SOMEONE WERE to ask me what I ordered for dinner, I'd tell them I don't have a fucking clue. I ate it all. I finished the wine in my glass, but I don't remember any of it.

I've spent the last two hours lost to the charms of Raelyn.

We talked about my process. She wanted to know where I find inspiration and if I've ever doubted my work.

I have no idea where the question came from, but I answered honestly. The doubt has given way to confidence, but there are still moments when I stand back and wonder why the hell anyone would pay a premium price for a tangle of twisted metal that I created and named.

The questions are in my corner now as she inspects the dessert menu.

"When was your last relationship, Raelyn?"

Her gaze drifts from the menu to my face. "Eight months ago."

I wait for more, but her eyes wander back to the feast of treats. Clearing my throat, I go on. "Tell me about him."

She sets the menu down. "Why?"

Because I'm a nosy bastard who wants to know every detail about the man who let her get away.

"I'm curious," I answer honestly.

She studies me for a moment. "Do things like that matter to you?"

"Things like what?" I play the dumb card. It's not a move I make often, but I want to see if she's the least bit interested in my past.

Running her fingertip around the rim of the wineglass in front of her, she shrugs. "How many? What were they like? Did any of them kiss better than you?"

Since we're heading down this path, I want answers to all of the questions. "How many lovers have you had?"

Coyly dipping her chin, she smiles. "Enough."

"Enough?" I chuckle.

"Enough to know whether a man is good or bad in bed."

My brows rise because I'm genuinely surprised by the answer. "Fair enough. Am I right to assume that I'm not going to get a straight answer about what they were like?"

"You're correct." She leans back in her chair.

Every move she makes is as sensual as it is graceful. She has to be a dream in bed.

"The kiss." I slide a finger over my bottom lip. "How was the kiss today?"

"Our kiss?" she asks with a soft laugh.

She's teasing me, or some other lucky bastard had a taste of her lips today. If that's true, I'll run him out of town by the end of tonight.

"It was perfection," she purrs. "All of our kisses today were a dream."

"Tonight they'll be better."

"I don't think that's even possible." She drags her top teeth over her bottom lip. "How can it be better?"

I lean across the table. Lowering my voice, I stare into her eyes. "Because I'll be kissing you in all the places I've been craving to taste."

———

I HAD to sit still through dessert while Raelyn ate a piece of cheesecake as if it was the sweetest thing ever to touch her tongue.

Even with my linen napkin in my lap, I was sure the server would notice I was hard as nails. He gave me a smirk before he turned back around to glance at Raelyn.

Who the fuck can blame him? She's every man's dream.

"Are you going to ask me to spend the night with you?" she questions.

I level my gaze on her face. "Is that a real question?"

A laugh bubbles out of her. "Yes."

"If I ask, will you say yes?"

"Ask and find out." She sips the last of the wine in her glass.

I reach for her hand and cradle it in mine. "If you feel comfortable spending the night with me, I'd be the happiest man alive, but if you're not, I'll settle for an hour or two of kissing in my hot studio. Clothing optional, of course."

"Let's start with kissing."

I'm game for anything that involves my mouth on her body. "Are you ready to leave?"

She drags her fingertip over her bottom lip. "I think I'm as ready as I'll ever be."

CHAPTER TWENTY

RAELYN

WE'RE LOCKED in a heated embrace the moment the door to his studio closes. I wind my fingers through Calder's hair as he tenderly cradles me in his arms.

He groans into our kiss. "Jesus, woman, you can kiss."

I smile at that. I like that he's satisfied with just kissing me for now. I want more. I know he does too. I can feel his erection pressing against me.

I know he's large. I sense it when he rocks against me. Part of me wants nothing more than to drop to my knees, unzip his pants, and take him in my mouth.

He inches me toward the wall until my back rests against it.

I moan. "I want to."

He stops mid-kiss. Drawing back, he searches my eyes with his. "You want to what?"

"Touch more of you," I answer breathlessly.

His suit jacket and shirt are on the floor before I can

register a thought. His hands drop to his pants. The belt leaves the loops with a sharp hissing sound. When his fingers reach the button of his pants, he gazes into my eyes. "Tell me when to stop."

I don't say anything.

His pants hit the floor, along with his shoes and socks leaving him in only a pair of black boxer briefs.

I'm not ashamed to stare. I want this man. I want to touch every part of him.

Before Calder can say a word, I slide my coat from my shoulders. My dress follows, falling into a puddle of black silk at my feet.

I feel his gaze burning a path over my body.

His breath hitches when his eyes hone in on the pink lace bow in the center of my black bra. "Jesus, Raelyn. You're so goddamn beautiful."

He reaches his hand out to touch me but pulls it back.

"I need you to set the pace." He chuckles. "If you leave it to me, I'll be on my knees with my tongue gliding over your pussy in the next two seconds."

Everything is happening so fast, but it feels right. So right that it's overwhelming.

Touching my lips to his for a tender kiss, I whisper. "You set the pace, Calder."

"Fuck," he hisses out between clenched teeth as he lowers himself down my body, kissing a path to my core.

———

HE TAKES his time charting a path over the skin of my inner thigh with feather-light kisses.

I'm on fire. Every part of me is waiting in anticipation. I tremble when his hands tug on my panties.

"Grab my shoulders to steady yourself, " he says, looking up at me. "Hold onto me if you need to."

I reach one hand down to rest on his shoulder as he lowers the lace down my thighs.

I close my eyes when I hear his breath hitch. A muted, "*fuck me*," leaves his lips before he glides his tongue over my cleft.

He licks me slowly at first, savoring everything. The sounds of pleasure falling from his lips set me closer and closer to the edge.

I need to come under his touch, but I don't want this to end.

He slides his finger over the tip of my clit, stirring my need even more. "You're so goddamn breathtaking, Raelyn. Every part of you is beautiful."

I sigh as I twist both hands in his hair. "Taste me. Take me."

He dives into me, his tongue trailing a hot path over my folds until it hones in on the swollen nub. He circles my clit, again and again, luring sounds from deep inside of me that I've never heard before.

I cry out as I race toward my release.

"That's it," he whispers. "Let me hear you come. Let me taste it. I want to feel it."

Two of his thick fingers dive into my channel as he takes my clit between his lips.

It's all too much. I can barely breathe as I fly over the edge into a soul-crushing orgasm that leaves me panting for breath and at the same time craving more.

My hands dart to my face to cover myself. Tears are pricking my eyes. I know my skin must be flushed.

I sense Calder moving. I feel the brush of the head of his cock against my leg. "Look at me, Raelyn."

I catch a fleeting breath and then another. "It's so much."

He grabs my hands, dragging them far enough down that my eyes are visible. "Open your eyes and look at me," he demands.

I crack open one eyelid and then the other. His face is flushed, his lips wet. It's his eyes that I can't stop staring at. I see the need I feel reflected at me. He wants me. I see it. I sense it. I feel it to my very core.

"I need to fuck you," he spits the words out slowly. "I'm aching to be inside of you."

"Condom," I whisper.

He nods before he bends to pick up his pants. He rifles in the pocket, tossing keys and his wallet aside before he produces a foil packet. He slides off his boxer briefs, rips open the package, and sheaths his cock.

I glance down.

"I'm so goddamn ready for this," he says before he presses his lips to the center of my bra.

Reaching behind me, I undo the clasp. My breasts fall out as the straps slide down my arms before the bra tumbles to our feet.

He takes one breast in his hand, roughly rubbing the pad of his thumb over my engorged nipple. "You want this. Tell me you do."

I nod. "So much."

With that, he spins me around, drags his hand over my ass, and pushes my feet apart with his foot.

I brace against the wall. My breathing is heavy and labored. My heart is pounding so hard that it's all I can hear until he guides the tip of his erection over my wetness. "Feel that, Raelyn? That's pure desire. That's how badly I want to feel your tight pussy grip my cock."

I let out a moan that trails when he slides into me with one long, painfully slow thrust.

I inch my ass toward him. "Calder."

His hand circles my neck from behind. He tugs me closer, planting kisses over my shoulders. "You're so goddamn tight. Fuck, it's so good."

He starts his thrusts on a rhythm. When his fingers find my pussy, and he thrums his fingertip over my clit, I fall apart. I moan, whisper words of devotion, and scream as he fucks me harder and harder until we both come.

CHAPTER TWENTY-ONE

CALDER

I CARRIED her to my bed after we fucked. She insisted she could walk, but I wasn't about to let her steal the pleasure of caring for her.

I washed her pussy with a warm cloth, gave her a bottle of water, and fed her slices of oranges before she fell asleep in the middle of my bed.

After I went downstairs to gather our things, I crawled in next to her and slept.

I slept for hours with her body curved against mine and her cheek resting on my chest.

The warmth of her body soothed me in a way I've never felt before. I woke up in awe that this is my reality.

The temptation to leave her alone to rest was strong because I wanted to go down and work on the sculpture for her sister. I wanted to use the inspiration that has flooded me from the inside out to create something as beautiful as the woman who shared her body with me.

If I weren't a cynic, I'd think I'm falling in love with her.

I'm smart enough to know that feelings set that deep inside of one's soul take time and patience. If there's a snowball's chance in hell that one day Raelyn will love me, I'll wait. I know that if I see her more and spend time understanding the woman she is, I'll be lost to her forever.

Her phone starts ringing in her purse.

She stirs next to me. Her right eye opens a crack. "Are you real?"

I chuckle. "Very real."

She moves her legs as the phone rings on. "I'm sore in places I've never been before."

"I'll take that as a compliment."

Both of her deep brown eyes lock on my face. "You should. That was incredible."

I lean over to kiss her forehead. "That was the beginning."

As her phone quiets, she glances at her purse. "What time is it?"

"Early," I answer. "It's just past six."

"I don't have to be at work until eight tonight, so that gives us time for more." A light-sounding giggle follows those words.

"Time for more?" I ask with a pop of both my brows.

She drags her thumb over my bottom lip. "This and ..."

"That?" I grab my erection through the thin sheet covering us.

She gazes down. "Yes, that."

Her phone rings again, and concern drapes her expression.

Before she can ask, I move to grab her purse. "I'll get that for you."

Her hand dives inside the moment I've placed it on the

bed next to her. She glances at the screen. "Amsterdam? Who would be calling me from Amsterdam?"

"Someone who speaks Dutch?" I smile.

She returns my smile with a brighter one. "There's only one way to find out."

Her finger slides across the screen to connect the call. "This is Rae Walsh."

Staring at her, I try to register what she just said. My eyes drift to the painting on the wall behind her. Even though the room is darkened, I can see the painting clear as day in my mind's eye.

A beautiful blonde woman is sitting on a swing in the vast expanse of an empty field. Her face is upturned toward the sun as the light blankets her in a halo. The colors are a muted mix of greens and blues except for the woman. She's wearing a white dress. Her golden hair is caught in the wind created from the swing's movements.

It's calming. It's soothing. It has fed my soul for almost a year.

When I asked the woman I bought it from who painted it, she pointed at the messy signature. All I could make out was a rounded R followed by Walsh.

She said the name of the artist was Ray Walsh. Eleni Melo offered me the painting when I stopped by her compound in Brazil. I was on vacation alone. She was trying to shove one of her sculptures on me in exchange for a night spent together. I turned down both but made an offer on the painting that was sitting on an easel nearby.

Her assistant, Ray, was off running an errand. She assured me it wasn't a problem for me to buy it. "Ray will appreciate it," she said.

No. *Rae* will appreciate it.

My beautiful Raelyn.

I hope to hell she got every last cent of the five thousand dollars I handed to Eleni in exchange for the painting.

I turn back to look at Raelyn as she talks to whoever is on the other end of the phone. I finally listen to her side of the conversation.

"I'm very interested in the position," she says, picking at a loose thread on the sheet covering her body. "I'd love to do a video chat. Can we set that up for tomorrow?"

I want to grab the phone from her hand and fist it in mine. I selfishly want her in New York, not in a place where an ocean separates us.

"I can start in a few weeks." She lets out a heavy breath. "I'm visiting my sister and her husband right now and working on a special project."

Her eyes find mine. "A very special sculpture."

She trails her fingers over my bare shoulder as she listens intently.

"I'll speak to you soon and thank you for the opportunity."

Ending the call, she lowers the phone to the bed. "Where were we?"

I was falling in love with you. You're making plans to fly away.

Fly Away.

It's the name of the sculpture that connected us that night. It's the same thing that will tear her from my life.

CHAPTER TWENTY-TWO

RAELYN

CALDER DOESN'T SAY a word as I tuck my phone back into my purse. I watch him closely, noting that his breathing has quickened and his jaw has tightened.

"You look like you're ready to devour me or spank me," I joke.

His lips don't move. A chuckle doesn't escape him. He just stares through me.

"Calder." I reach forward to stroke my fingers over his cheek. "Kiss me."

He does. It's intense, passionate, and with an arm behind my back, he lowers me to the bed. "Make love with me, Rae."

Rae. He's never called me that.

"I like that," I whisper.

He swallows hard. "Rae Walsh."

"Calder Frost." I smile. "Now that we've affirmed our identities, we're free and clear to make love."

He lowers his head to rest it on my breast. "Do you believe in fate?"

I twist a lock of his hair around my finger. "I do."

"Me too," he whispers. "I didn't before I met you, but you changed that."

I close my eyes as I feel his lips trail a path over the sensitive skin of my breast. When he flicks his tongue over my nipple, I shiver. "You're such a good lover."

I expect a witty comeback, but he has other ideas. He kisses my other nipple. He's less tender. His touch is more aggressive, but it draws another moan from somewhere deep inside me.

I reach down to cradle his head in my hands. Inching his chin up, I find his eyes with mine. "Last night and today have been incredible."

"It's not over yet." He pauses. "I don't want it to be over yet."

I don't either, and it's not just the sex. I don't want whatever is happening between us to be over, but soon I might leave for Amsterdam to start a new job, he'll fall back into his routine, and we'll become fond memories to each other.

His lips press kisses over my stomach to my hipbone. He tugs on the sheet that is covering me until my body is bare.

"Why does it feel like I've known you forever?" he asks as he gazes up at me.

I feel that too. It makes no sense, but I feel a sense of peace when I'm with him that I've never felt before.

I moan when his hand trails over my skin to my core. He parts my legs before he drags his fingers over my tender flesh. "You're not leaving this bed, Raelyn."

"Until we make love again?" I whisper.

He doesn't answer. His body tells me what I need to know. For now, at this moment, he wants me as much as I want him, and I can't ask for more even though I want his every tomorrow.

————

I REST my head against Calder's chest as he massages shampoo into my hair. "This is the best."

He laughs. The sound vibrates through him. "Better than what we just did?"

Shaking my head, I answer honestly. "No. That was better than the best."

We spent two hours slowly exploring each other. He got me off with his mouth before I took him in mine. With a slow groan and a twist of his hands in my tangled hair, he came on my tongue.

Twenty minutes later, he was buried deep inside of me, whispering words that soothed my soul.

He told me I'm beautiful. He called me his sunshine. He swore he'd never felt anything as good as us together.

Warm water rushes over me as he rinses the shampoo away.

Conditioner is next. He runs his finger over my hair, coating it with a cream that smells incredible. It's masculine and strong, just like him.

I smile, knowing that a woman isn't comfortable enough to leave her things here. Everything in this loft is Calder's. It's only his.

He brushes his fingers over my face chasing away any wayward drops of water.

We switch positions so he can run the water over his head. He washes his hair in a rush before he pushes it back from his forehead.

Resting both hands on his chest, I stare at him.

"You're looking at me," he accuses with his eyes closed.

"How could I not?" I confess. "You're a dream come true."

"You are."

I tap my fingers on his chest. "You can't steal my thunder like that. Accept the compliment, Frost."

His eyes pop open. "I will, but I meant what I said, Raelyn. You are a dream come true."

They are sweet words men whisper to women when they're satiated. When their muscles are sore from pleasure, and they're drained of their strength in the best way possible, they soften. Men say what sits in their hearts when they feel fulfilled.

It may be fleeting, but it feeds something inside of me.

"I need to show you something." He scrubs his face with his hand. "I can't explain it, Raelyn. Maybe I don't need to. Maybe it will all make sense to you."

Dread settles inside of me, tugging at my heart. "What do you need to show me?"

He grabs my arms to shift our positions. Tilting my head back, so the hot water washes away the conditioner, he kisses my forehead. "Let's finish this, and then you'll see."

I close my eyes and wish. I wish for this to be the beginning of the rest of my life, not the end of what might have been.

CHAPTER TWENTY-THREE

CALDER

I HAVE TO DO THIS. I need to see her face to know for sure that Raelyn is the artist behind that masterpiece hanging in my bedroom.

I should have asked before we made love. I was tempted to stop her on her way to the shower. It would have only taken a turn of her waist to direct her eyes to the painting, but I didn't do it.

I had to let my shock settle before I let this dream slip through my fingers.

Maybe the Ray Walsh who painted this is a kid who has talent beyond his years. Or it could be a man who has spent years honing his craft until he captured the beauty of his lover on a sunny, summer afternoon.

My heart is telling me that the woman I'm toweling dry is the one who placed each brush stroke on that canvas. It's her quirky signature in the corner. The shakiness of it reflects how unaware she was of her talent when she completed the piece.

"Tell me that what you are about to show me won't hurt me." A crooked smile accompanies those words. She's trying to find something to anchor her feelings, so I give her that, to the extent that I can.

"I pray it doesn't hurt you," I say honestly. "Please know that I would walk on a fire barefoot before I'd ever hurt you."

Her gaze drops to the sweatpants I'm wearing. "Can you get my dress?"

I reach for my navy blue robe hanging on a hook on the bathroom door. I wrap it around her, and even though her arms get lost in the length of the sleeves, she smiles. "I like this."

"I do too," I confess. "Come with me?"

I offer her my shaking hand. She takes it in both of hers.

With the sound of my heart pounding in my chest, I open the bathroom door to head back into the bedroom, tugging gently on her hand as she follows me.

Once we reach the bedroom, I position her so her back is to the painting. I need to preface this with my story. With the comfort I've found with her and with what I believe to be a self-portrait that she created.

"Do you know Eleni Melo, Rae?"

Her eyes widen. Her teeth latch onto the corner of her bottom lip. With a nod, she whispers, "I worked for her for a year."

"When was that?"

"Did you sleep together?" Her bottom lip trembles. "Is that it? Do you have a picture of the two of you together? If that's what you want to show me, I don't want to see it."

I reach for her chin. "No. It's not that. It's nothing like that."

Her eyes search mine. "What is it? Just show me, Calder. Please."

The plea in her tone cuts through me. "I need you to know that I had no idea that you were the artist before I met you."

"The artist?" she parrots my words back to me. "I'm just an artist. Sometimes I wonder if I should be."

My gaze falls to the painting behind her. "You are an artist. You are the most talented artist I've ever known."

Tears fill her eyes. "You don't have to say that. You don't know my work, Calder. All you've seen are the broken pieces of a Christmas ornament."

I rest my lips against her forehead. "I've seen so much more than that."

She looks up at me. "What do you mean?"

I slowly spin her around. "I bought that from Eleni a year ago. I had to. It spoke to me in a way I can't explain."

Her head falls into her hands as a sob escapes her. "You have it? You have my painting?"

I round her until I'm directly in front of her. "I've always had it."

With her shaking hands resting against my chest, tears race down her cheeks. "I thought it was stolen. I thought I'd never see it again."

The urge to call Eleni is strong, but I resist. She can go to hell. It's Raelyn who needs me. She needs all of me.

"It's been here, in your bedroom, all this time?"

I nod. "It's been here. I think it's been waiting for you, just like I have."

———

HER GAZE HASN'T LEFT the painting since I held her as she cried. To know that she believed her work was stolen when it was sold right out from under her makes my blood boil.

Raelyn deserved better than this.

"That's the first painting I ever did of myself," she whispers.

I wrap my arms around her from behind. "It's you in a field. There's happiness in your surroundings, but sorrow in your solace."

Her body shakes with a silent sob, so I bring her closer. I drop my lips to her ear. "I've got you. I'm here."

"You see it, don't you?" she asks. "The loneliness. The fear. You see it all, don't you?"

"I feel it." I kiss her cheek. "I feel the depth of your emotions when I look at the painting. That's why I had to have it."

For the first time, she turns from the painting to face me. "You kept it safe for me."

I nod. "I did."

"There were always people going in and out of Eleni's compound. She said it was taken when she wasn't looking. She swore that she spoke to the police about it, but the painting was never recovered."

"I gave her five thousand dollars for it." I wince. "She told me the artist would be grateful that I bought it."

Raelyn's hands rest in the center of her chest. "I had no idea."

Nodding my head, I look into her eyes. "I thought you were a guy. I thought Ray with a 'y' painted this. I searched for him online and came up empty."

That lures a small laugh from her. "I'm not a guy."

I rake her from head-to-toe. "Clearly."

"You didn't make the connection when we met?" she questions.

I'm ashamed to admit it, but I need to come clean, so I do. "Until tonight, I thought your name was Raelyn Jones."

This time the laugh is heartier, more joyful. It blooms somewhere deep inside of her and spills out. "Why would you think that?"

"This is fucking embarrassing," I confess. "I assumed your surname was the same as Dexie's. She wasn't wearing a ring when we met at the auction."

"She's pregnant." She holds her hands in front of her stomach. "Very pregnant."

"You don't need a husband to have a baby," I point out with a chuckle.

"True," she agrees. "I meant that because she's pregnant, her fingers are swollen. She can't wear her rings until after the baby arrives."

I smile at the way her voice changes when she says the word '*baby*.'

"So all of this time, you thought I was Raelyn Jones?"

Nodding, I close my eyes. "Guilty as charged."

Her hand on my chin soothes me. I open my eyes to find her staring at me. "You know me now."

"I do." I want to know more, but I don't know if I'll get that chance. Maybe I need to create that chance, so the best thing in my life doesn't get on an airplane and move to another continent.

"Do you have other paintings, Raelyn? If you do, I'd love to see them."

CHAPTER TWENTY-FOUR

RAELYN

I HOLD my breath as Calder studies the images of my paintings on my phone's screen. He hasn't said a word since I gave him the phone and told him to scroll through them.

Each time I complete a painting, I take a picture of it.

Other than the painting hanging in Dexie's townhouse and this one in Calder's bedroom, only two of my paintings belong to someone other than me. Both went to a woman I met at the airport on my way to London.

She was sitting next to me in the terminal as we waited to board our flight. The fact that she was nosy paid off for me because once she caught a glimpse of the photos of my paintings, she asked where to purchase one. That one became two, and with an exchange of our contact details and a few hundred dollars cash in my palm, we agreed that I'd have them shipped to her flat in London.

Dexie handled those arrangements for me.

As the plane left the runway that day, I cried tears of

happiness. It was the first time I felt pride bloom in my chest. Someone not related to me liked my work enough to want to buy not one but two of my creations.

"Where do you store these paintings?" Calder's head pops up with the question.

We're sitting on the edge of his bed. Calder is still shirtless, and I'm wrapped in his robe. I've never been more comfortable in my life.

"Dexie's townhouse," I say. "Rocco, her husband, knows a lot about art, so he takes care of them."

He flashes me a smile. "He takes care of them?"

Laughing, I push his shoulder. "You know what I mean. He stores them in a room. It's climate-controlled and dark."

Nodding, he glances back at my phone. "How many in total are there?"

I look down at the screen before my gaze levels on him. "More than a hundred by now. I lost count."

He shifts until he's facing me directly. With a touch of his finger to my chin, he exhales. "Rae, these should be in a gallery."

I study his face. "They should be?"

"Do you know how much just one of these paintings is worth?"

I shrug. I've never put much thought into that. "Rocco gave me two thousand dollars when he bought one, but he's family, so he was extra generous. A woman I met on my way to London gave me three hundred for two."

"Rocco and that woman both got a hell of a good deal." He points at my painting on the wall. "I did too."

I brush my hand over my forehead. "Are you saying you think more of my paintings are worth thousands of dollars?"

"I think all of them are."

I stare at his lips. "You work in metal. You're a sculptor."

"And a lover of art," he adds. "I know brilliance when I see it, Raelyn. You don't need to be working for anyone. You're sitting on a goldmine."

If he's right, this is life-changing. I can stay in New York. I can be here when my sister has her baby. I can rent an apartment and a studio in the city I love. I can be close to Calder.

"I think we should take a couple of your paintings to a gallery I know and have them appraised."

"When?" I spit out.

"I'll make a few calls." He picks up his phone from the nightstand. "Let's get it done this week."

"I can't believe this is happening." My voice cracks. "Maybe I don't have to wait so long for all of my dreams to come true."

He leans closer to brush a soft kiss over my lips. "Maybe they're coming true now."

———

I'M HALFWAY through finishing an ornament when Calder comes racing down the stairs from his loft.

After we arranged for me to drop off two paintings at a gallery in the West Village tomorrow, he got a call from his sister.

She called her engagement off and needed his advice.

I listened as he calmed her and told her that one day the right man would walk into her life when she least expects it. As his gaze drifted to mine, he remarked to Magnolia that she might run into a stranger on the sidewalk and that man could change everything for her.

After that call, he gathered me in his arms and made love to me.

It was tender and pure. We held each other tightly as we

fell from the high. I never wanted to leave his arms, but as he drifted back to sleep, I crawled out of bed and came down here to work.

I needed a moment alone to process everything that's happened to me since I first saw Calder on the sidewalk the night we crashed into one another.

This could be my life.

I could work on my craft full-time instead of assisting someone else as they do.

I can live in the same city as my sister, her husband, and the baby.

I can see Calder.

I can keep falling in love with him.

I gaze down at the ornament in my hands. Paint streaks cover my fingertips and palms. I'm still wearing the blue robe that my lover draped around me, and deep inside my chest, my heart is beating so hard I almost can't breathe.

I thought it took endless hours of talking and months of understanding another human being to fall in love with them.

But I feel it already. The embers are there, laying a base for what is to come.

This is the beginning of love, and I never want it to end.

"What do you have there?" Calder rests his hands on my shoulders. "Is that the ornament I ordered?"

I glance back and up at his handsome face. "I canceled your order."

He chuckles. "Why the hell would you do that? I was prepared to pay you three times what you normally make on one. Did you forget?"

I move to stand so I can face him. He's dressed in a pair of navy blue pants and a white button-down shirt. A suit coat is draped over his forearm.

"I didn't forget." I sigh. "I plan on making you a special ornament for Christmas. It will be my gift to you."

His eyes narrow. "You're doing that for me, Raelyn?"

I'd do anything for you.

Those words don't leave my mouth. I'm scared I'm falling faster than he is.

Nodding, I wave my paint-stained hands in the air. "I need to wash up. It looks like you're on your way out. I should go home for a few hours before I report back here for work tonight."

"Stay," he insists with a soft kiss to my mouth. "I won't be gone long. I'm on the board of an art exhibition for teens set to launch next summer. We're meeting today to firm up some of the details."

His generosity knows no limits. He's proven time and time again that he's not the selfish man I met on the sidewalk when snow draped the city.

"When I get back, I want to talk."

"About?" I ask hesitantly.

"Us," he answers succinctly. "There's something here that feels rare. I don't know if it's the same for you. I realize you had plans to move to Amsterdam, and maybe I'm jumping ahead of myself, but…"

I interrupt him with a kiss on the mouth. "It's the same. Let's talk about us tonight."

His hand moves to cup my cheek before he gives me another kiss. This one is longer. His touch is softer. "I'll be back in a few hours."

"I'll be gone by then," I say. "There's something important I need to take care of today. I'm going to call Eleni. I need to. I don't care about the money, but I trusted her and she needs to know that she shattered that."

His eyes search mine for a clue. "If you need backup, I'm an Uber ride away."

"I need to handle this alone." I straighten. "It's important that I do."

With one last press of his lips to my forehead, he closes his eyes. "You're my favorite person, Raelyn."

I bite back my emotions as I close my eyes too. "You're mine."

CHAPTER TWENTY-FIVE

CALDER

I SPENT the day spreading cheer in the world. That's a first for me. Instead of rushing around Manhattan frustrated with all the people getting in my way, I smiled at everyone I passed.

I bought coffee for a group of college kids who stopped by their favorite café to load up on caffeine.

Then, I did something that I swore I never would do. I watched my grandpa do it when I was a nine-year-old kid. Christmas was approaching, and instead of giving gifts to my older brother Lennox, Magnolia, and me, he took us down to the grocery store and made us watch him pay for other people's food.

At the time, I was angry with him.

I wanted a building block set, but he wanted my siblings and me to understand that fate doesn't cast the same shadow on everyone.

Lennox got the message loud and clear. He used the good

that thrives within him to keep the tradition going. Somewhere in this city, he's probably standing in a grocery store, wearing an expensive suit, and playing Santa to everyone.

He's a lawyer with the heart of a saint.

Magnolia and I are still getting there. I'm determined to be a better person because I want Raelyn to be proud of me.

That's not to say that I haven't sprinkled my wealth around and planted a few seeds in the form of scholarships or donations to worthwhile charities. But, there's a different peace that settles inside someone when they help a stranger who is down on their luck.

I turn the key in my studio's lock, hoping that Rae made it back before me. For someone who craved solace a few weeks ago, I never want to be alone again.

I need to temper that need. If I come at Raelyn with the full force of my emotions, I'll scare her the fuck away.

I slide the door open and blink twice.

This can't possibly be real.

A Christmas tree is set up in the middle of my studio. It's decorated with sparkling white lights. I step in and slide the door shut behind me.

Music is playing softly. It's a Christmas carol that I recognize from the days I used to sing it with my family before opening gifts and diving into our feast.

My gaze shifts to Raelyn.

She's standing next to the tree. She's dressed in red. It's not the pantsuit she had on the night we were formally introduced. This is a dress. The fabric shimmers as the lights from the tree bounce off it.

I approach her with measured, heavy steps. With her arms outstretched, she walks toward me. We meet halfway as I pick her up and spin her in a circle. The skirt of her dress floats around her legs.

"You look like an angel, Rae."

Her eyes flutter shut before she opens them again. "I hope this is all right?"

Glancing around the studio, I see a table set with a white cloth, two tall white candles, plates, wine glasses, and a pizza box in the middle.

"Dexie told me that's the best pizza in Brooklyn." She scrunches her nose. "I may have had a sample bite. I think she's right."

Laughing, I kiss her softly. "I can't believe you did all of this."

"We're celebrating." She moves to slide my jacket off. "Get comfortable, Calder."

"How comfortable?" I perk a brow.

"Take off the tie. Leave the rest on for now."

I pout, which lures a laugh from her.

"What are we celebrating?" I question as I gaze into her dark brown eyes.

"My lost painting is found." She smiles. "I couldn't have asked for a better gift."

I lift my brows. "We should celebrate the fact that I found the artist behind that masterpiece. I never thought I would."

"You were looking for some guy named Ray," she points out. "If you kept doing that, you never would have found me."

"You would have found me." I surprise myself with the words.

"Fate would have shown me the way here."

I nod. "I like to think that."

She kisses me. It's slow, and as she breathes me in, my heart races. "I'm the luckiest man in Manhattan."

"You wanted to talk about us." Her breath flows over my cheek. "What about us, Calder?"

I've thought about this conversation all day. I've searched for the right words and rehearsed what I want to say over and over.

"I'm crazy about you," I admit. "Don't ask me how I can feel this much this quickly, but it's happening."

Her eyes stay trained on mine. "I'm just as crazy about you."

"I don't know what tomorrow is going to bring, and stop me if you think I'm pushing or scaring you." I pause to catch my breath.

"You're not scaring me."

"Yet," I joke. "I'm only getting started."

She waits for me to go on.

"I know Amsterdam is still on the table, and even if the appraisals on your paintings come back high, and I'm confident they will, I know you probably crave adventure." I stare into her eyes. "I'm falling hard for you, Rae, and if your journey takes you across the ocean, I want to visit you. Hell, I want to be with you often as I can because this feeling that's inside of me is new. I can't get enough of it or you."

Tears pool in the corners of her eyes.

"I'm not asking you for anything." I cup her face in my hands. "I just want a chance. I want to see where this can go, and hell, if it goes the way I think it will, I want a future with you. I want my entire future to be with you."

I suck in a breath because that is not the fucking speech I prepared. This came from my heart. Laid bare and pounding in my chest, I said what I felt for the first time in my life.

"I'm not going to Amsterdam," she whispers. "I don't care if I have to work three jobs like my mom did or paint Christmas ornaments for the rest of my life. I don't want to go. I want to stay and see if my heart is right because it's telling me that you are my tomorrow, Calder. I know it's too soon, but I feel that we were always meant to be. We just took a few detours before we found each other in that snowstorm."

As if on cue, snow starts falling outside.

Rae glances at one of the massive windows that overlook Manhattan. "I belong here with you, with Dex, with her baby. I want New York City to be my home."

I test fate and blurt out what I've wanted since I saw her on the sidewalk. "I want this to be your home. This studio, the loft, all of it."

She glances around. "It feels like home, but…"

My stomach clenches in a knot. "Look, if I went too hard, forgive me. I know it's soon."

"I'll stay with Dex and Rocco until the baby is born, and maybe after that, we can talk about me moving in?"

It's enough for me. It's more than I deserve. "Agreed."

"Are you hungry?" She asks, eyeing the pizza box.

"For you, yes." I slide my hands down her waist. "But, we'll eat pizza, and then I'm carrying you to our bed."

Her smile tells me that it will always be our bed. It's the place we'll make love, plan our future, and find our inspiration.

With her head resting on my shoulder, we both stare out at the night sky and the falling snow. "You make me happy, Calder Frost."

"If that's all I do in life, I'll die fulfilled with my purpose."

She glances up at me. "I'm glad you broke my balls."

I huff out a laugh. "I am too."

CHAPTER TWENTY-SIX

RAELYN

MY BREATH HITCHES in the darkness when I feel Calder slide his nude body over mine.

We both left the table as soon as we finished our pizza dinner. He chased me up the stairs, finally grabbing hold of me just as I made it to the bed.

My dress was pulled off with his strong hands before he knelt between my legs and brought me to the edge over and over. I clawed at his hair as he tasted me. His lips sucked my clit. His fingers stroked my pussy, and when I finally did come, he lapped at me, sending me into another dizzying orgasm.

He whispered that he wanted me to sleep because he was aching to fuck me.

"Raelyn," he says my name with his lips pressed against my breast. "Your body was made just for me."

I believe that.

He knows how to touch me, kiss me, and fuck me. I feel

things when I'm with him that I didn't think I'd ever feel. It reaches beyond the bliss of an orgasm. When I come with Calder, I feel it in every part of me.

He glides his fingers over my folds. "You're wet."

"I was dreaming about you," I whisper.

He lets out a deep laugh. "Never stop that."

"Never."

His arm slides beneath me, moving me so he can take me the way he needs to. It's the way I want. Rough, hard, passionately.

I cry out when he pushes into me. I moan when the deep-seated guttural sound comes out of him as he thrusts again and again.

"Calder." His name falls from my lips in a silent vow.

"So good." He pumps again and then again, pushing me toward another release.

I grab hold of his shoulders, force him closer to me and kiss him.

"I adore you," he murmurs against my mouth. "So fucking much."

With his hand wrapped around my neck, he kisses me hard, leaving an imprint on my soul that I know will be there forever.

———

TWO HOURS LATER, with his blue robe on, I'm sitting on a bench next to one of the windows in the studio. The snow has stopped, but the blanket of white covering the roofs of the buildings of Manhattan is still there.

I wouldn't call it a winter wonderland, but it could be the scene from a dream. I stare out at it, determined to save it all to memory so that it will find its way, in some form, into my art.

"This is a fucking vision."

I look over when I see Calder at the foot of the stairs. He was asleep when I left him. I wanted to finish my Christmas gift for him.

As he approaches, his gaze drifts to the tree. I can see the moment he spots my gift. It's hanging in the center. It's the only thing on the tree, other than the string of white lights I draped over the branches earlier.

"That's for you, Calder."

"For me?" His hand jumps to the center of his bare chest.

He put on a pair of jeans before he came down to the studio. He looks beautiful with his hair messed from my hands, and his lips swollen from my kisses.

I stand and approach him. "I've been working on it whenever I had a chance."

I watch as he leans in to get a better look at the ornament.

His smile gives way to a laugh. "Is that us?"

I nod. "It's us."

He cradles the ornament in his hand. "That's you with your wool coat. I'm there with my gray scarf. Is that a coffee cup in my hand?"

"Look what's in my hands."

He does before turning to face me. "It's the bag of balls, isn't it?"

I step closer and reach for the ornament. Carefully removing it from the tree, I look up at him. "Open your hands."

He does. He stretches his hands out while I place the ornament in them.

With a run of my hand over his cheek, I whisper. "Turn it over."

His eyes catch mine. "This is exquisite. It's perfect, Raelyn."

"The other side has something on it too," I whisper, trying to control my emotion.

He carefully rolls it in his hands until the other side of the globe comes into view. "Fuck. Wow, Rae. This is fucking everything."

It is.

It's my painting laid out on a smaller, breakable canvas. I'm there on the swing, with my hair flying in the wind and the vast field around me. There's something extra in this version of my self-portrait.

"That's me," Calder says with his voice breaking. "I'm pushing you on the swing."

His eyes meet mine.

We stare at each other, soaking in the pure magic of the moment and this life.

"I'm not alone anymore." I smile. "You're there with me."

"You'll never be alone again, Raelyn. I'll always be right beside you."

EPILOGUE

Raelyn

I CAREFULLY UNWRAP the gift from Rocco and Dexie as they watch. Calder is here too. Dexie invited him not just to unveil the sculpture in the foyer but so that my family could get to know the man I love.

It's still early, but I know this is love.

Calder knows too.

We haven't exchanged the words, but we're close.

"Vision is the perfect name for the sculpture," Rocco says as I continue prying tape from the gift box my sister handed me.

"It's fitting." Calder smiles at me. "Your wife had a vision, and I brought it to life. I was honored that she named it and I'm humbled that you see the beauty in it."

"I wish I would have seen the beauty in Rae's paintings."

Rocco crosses his legs as Dexie settles in next to her husband on the couch.

I stop what I'm doing to look at my brother-in-law. He's decked out in the T-shirt I got for him. He laughed when he saw BIL written across the front in pink letters. I laughed harder when I opened up a package that was labeled from Santa Claus.

Inside was a white button-down shirt. On the back, stamped in black letters, are the words Artistic Genius. On the front, in the same black ink, a small SIL is on the collar.

Rocco told me that I should take Santa's hint and wear it when I'm working in Calder's studio.

"You always supported my work, Rocco." I lean forward, resting my hand on Calder's knee. "If it wasn't for you buying that painting from me, I might not have pursued my passion."

He nods. "I'm always here if you need me."

"The same goes for me," Dexie chimes in. Her hand drops to the star-shaped pendant on the necklace she's wearing. It was my gift to her this Christmas. "Open it, Rae. I can't wait to see your face."

I glance over at Calder. Dressed in a dark suit, he looks every inch the gentleman. He was insistent that he wanted to wear a suit and tie to our Christmas Eve celebration. I didn't argue. Instead, I slipped into my red pantsuit because I know how much he loves it.

Finally, pulling the last piece of tape free, I open the rectangular box and peer inside.

"You got me an envelope?" I ask with a chuckle.

"I promise you there's something very special inside."

Curiosity sets my hands to work. I carefully rip open the envelope before sliding a single piece of white paper out.

Dexie jumps to the edge of the seat. "I'm freaking out. Open it."

Rocco laughs. "She's getting there. Give her a minute."

I take that minute to look at the faces of my family. I wish my mom could be here, but she's found someone this Christmas too. A doctor she works with invited her to have dinner at his home in Aspen. She took the chance because that's what we all need to do. Dive in headfirst, and hope that when you emerge from the murky waters, light will be waiting for you.

After I glance at Dexie and Rocco, I look at Calder again.

I stare at his brilliant blue eyes. They are the same eyes that held me captive during the snowstorm and gaze into mine when we make love.

They are the eyes of a gifted artist and a visionary. One day, I hope our children will have the same color eyes as Calder.

I take a breath and carefully open the paper in my lap.

At first, I can't register what I'm looking at, but then it hits me. My eyes fill with tears.

"Is this real?" I look at Dexie and Rocco. "This is real?"

Dex tears up. "When your nephew is born, we want you to be his godmother."

"It's a boy?" I ask. "You know that it's a boy?"

"We couldn't wait any longer." Rocco laughs. "We both thought we knew the gender, and we were right."

"What will his name be?" I ask as Calder grabs my hand.

"Bryant Walsh Jones." Dexie looks at Rocco. "Bryant Park holds a special place in Rocco's heart and Walsh, well that's us."

I smile. "It's perfect."

"What's perfect is that you'll be here to watch him grow

up." Rocco kisses Dexie's cheek. "The more family we have around us to love our boy, the better."

————

WE WALK into Calder's studio at ten minutes to midnight. Our evening was spent with my family. After we opened gifts with Dexie and Rocco, we crossed the street for a big meal with Rocco's family.

It was overwhelming in the most wonderful of ways. Calder felt comfortable. I could see it in the way he stepped into every conversation with ease. He smiled at me constantly, and when the evening was winding down, he helped Marti with the cleanup, insisting that he was going to create a sculpture for her birthday.

I know he will.

As he takes my coat from me, he feathers kisses over the back of my neck. "I love this pantsuit."

"You love my ass in this pantsuit," I counter.

"I love all of you in that pantsuit." I hear him take a breath. "I love you."

I turn to face him. "What?"

He smiles. "You heard me, but I'll say it a million times if need be. I love you, Raelyn Walsh."

Resting my hands on his chest, I look into his eyes. "I love you, Calder Frost."

He stares at me. His gaze travels my face as if he's seeing it for the first time.

"I want you to marry me one day."

The words don't scare me. They only offer comfort and hope. I know I belong with him. I know he's my destiny. "I want the same thing."

"Move in with me." He looks around the studio. "You're

here almost all of the time. Work here. Live here. Be here…with me."

Nodding, I don't hesitate as I answer. "I'll do it tomorrow."

Cradling my face, he kisses me softly. "You've made me happier than I deserve, Rae."

"You deserve every happiness life can offer. I hope I'll always be a part of that."

"Always," he says before another kiss. "I have a gift for you."

"I told you I don't want the painting back." I sigh. "We've talked about this, Calder. The painting is yours now."

"It's our painting," he corrects me.

"Our painting," I repeat.

"This is something else."

Calder has already given me so much. He listened when I complained about Eleni never answering my calls until she did. He sat next to me as I told her how devastating it was when she stole my painting. She sold it without my permission, and her only excuse was that she was drowning in debt at the time and needed a quick fix. She wired me the money since that call and sent a note wishing me well as if our past could be erased with scented stationery and a heart drawn in red ink in place of her signature.

Calder has also helped me understand the value of my work. The appraisals of my paintings were higher than either of us imagined they would be. Within a week, I had signed a contract to feature them at one gallery. The following week, another in Tribeca wanted to place four on display for sale.

"It's under the tree." He points at a box covered in gold wrapping paper. It's partially hidden beneath a tree branch.

I bend down to pick it up. It's heavier than I thought it would be so I push it at Calder. "Hold it while I open it."

"That would be my pleasure."

I stop and admire the way the light is framing his face. As gorgeous as he is on the outside, it's what's beneath the surface that makes me love him.

I pull the top of the box off and toss it on the floor.

Calder smiles. "I hope you like what's inside."

"It's coming from you, so it's perfect."

I look into the box. Pushing the gold tissue paper aside, I tilt my head to get a better look.

"I made it for you," Calder whispers. "For us and for the family we'll have one day."

I scoop both hands into the box and pull out a sculpture. It's breathtaking. I hold it in front of me, marveling at the beauty of it.

"It's an angel for the top of our tree." Calder takes it from me. "Do you see it, Rae? That's her face and her wings. Her halo is on top."

I stare at it, taking in each curve of the metal and every edge that's bent just enough so the light bounces off of it, giving it dimension.

Calder drags a chair from the corner, stands on it, and positions our angel at the top of our tree. When he jumps down, he nods his head, satisfied.

Curling his strong arms around me, he holds me next to him. "This is just the beginning of our life together. I'm going to ask you to marry me the day before Valentine's Day."

I smile. "Why the day before?"

"I'm different like that," he quips.

"I'll say yes."

He kisses me tenderly. "Every year we'll add something new to our tree. And when we have kids, we'll keep adding until one day we explain to them that during a snowstorm, fate brought us to each other, and it kept us together until the end of time."

"Every Christmas will be better than the last, Calder."

"It will." He looks into my eyes. "I promise you that, my love."

ALSO BY DEBORAH BLADON
& SUGGESTED READING ORDER

HUSH

BARE

WISH

SIN

LACE

THIRST

COMPASS

VERSUS

RUTHLESS

BLOOM

RUSH

CATCH

FROSTBITE

XOXO

HE LOVES ME NOT

BITTERSWEET

THANK YOU

Thank you for purchasing and downloading my book. I can't even begin to put to words what it means to me. If you enjoyed it, please remember to write a review for it. Let me know your thoughts! I want to keep my readers happy.

For more information on new series and standalones, please visit my website, www.deborahbladon.com. There are book trailers and other goodies to check out.

If you want to chat with me personally, please LIKE my page on Facebook. I love connecting with all of my readers because without you, none of this would be possible. www.facebook.com/authordeborahbladon

Thank you, for everything.

ABOUT THE AUTHOR

Deborah Bladon has never read a romance hero she didn't like. Her love for romance novels began when she was old enough to board the bus, library card in hand to check out the newest Harlequin paperbacks. She's a Canadian by heart, and by passport, but you can often spot her in New York City sipping a latte and looking for inspiration for her next story. Manhattan is definitely her second home.

She cherishes her family and believes that each day is a gift for writing, for reading, and for loving.

Printed in Great Britain
by Amazon